In My Brother's Name

I0521403

Wayland Smith

Blue Oranda Publishing
www.BlueOranda.com

Published by Blue Oranda Publishing
Copyright 2012 Wayland Smith

Cover Design by Heather Heckel
Some Cover Art © Jemaerca | Dreamstime.com

ISBN-13: 978-0615684994 (Blue Oranda Publishing)

ISBN-10: 0615684998

Dedication

To my wife, for tireless proof reading, boundless patience, and for managing to not wince when I keep asking things like "Hey, what do you think would happen if...."

Acknowledgments

To the Paragon City Writer's Group, for vastly improving this story.

Several Years Ago

Exact Date Classified

Gerry Franklin sat at his desk and smiled. Feelings of exhilaration, pride, accomplishment, and satisfaction raced through him. He hadn't been with the Bureau that long, but he had been fortunate in finding some good informants, one in particular. Working off information from this source, dubbed "Accountant," Franklin had very carefully built his case, and the months of work had paid off. Fadi Hadad, one of the top terrorists in the Middle East, the mastermind behind strikes against Americans in Saudi Arabia and Yemen, and rumored to be a confidant of Osama bin Laden himself, was this minute in a cell, not even knowing what hit him. Probably literally—the tranquilizer rifles they'd used to ensure the target was taken alive were loaded with a powerful sedative.

He leaned back in his cheap, government-issued chair, and contemplated the piles of paper on his equally uninspiring desk. Even the conquering hero had paperwork to do. He'd been receiving hand shakes, back slaps, high fives, and various congratulatory phone calls since the capture had been confirmed. There was talk already of promotion, and the young agent fervently hoped it was true. Maybe something with an actual office instead of this cubicle, away from Rhonda Jennings and her bizarre array of aroma-therapy oils. He'd tried to talk to the woman, but really, she just would NOT listen. And a real paycheck, so he and Marcie could get that place they'd been looking at in Vienna, outside Washington itself but within reach of the Metro system so he could commute in easily enough, leave the car for Marcie to take Veronica (Don't call me Ronnie, Daddy!) around to her never-ending array of plays, concerts, soccer games, and whatever else she'd decided to pursue. Their daughter was brilliant, but seemed equally interested in almost everything. Frighteningly, she was almost equally good at all her interests.

He suddenly leaned forward as the chair threatened to roll out from under him and dump him on the floor. Again. That had happened on his first day here, making an embarrassingly loud THUD as it had unceremoniously deposited him on the floor. When Rhonda had peered around the corner to ask if he was all right, he'd said "Sure, I just dropped a paperclip and was looking for it." It had been a lame lie, and he had known it almost as soon as he'd said it. That story had gone all around the office faster than news of free donuts in the conference room and, coupled with his attention to detail and making sure all his paper work was done near perfectly, had earned him the nickname "Paperclip," which he'd come to loathe with a passion. See who called him that after today!

Catching his balance, he smiled, remembering the brief call from Special Agent Jack Conroy, his mentor since nearly his first day out of the FBI Academy at Quantico. Skipping the expected greetings, as usual, his gravelly voice had come through the receiver, "Sounds like you did good, kid." Conroy had become almost a father figure for Gerry, and he was elated at the praise, although he tried hard to hide it. Conroy was a relic of another era, and seemed more like he should be a Texas Ranger in the old west than one of the FBI's better manhunters. The tall, grey-haired man looked like a farmer, talked like a hick, and hid one of the sharpest investigative minds Gerry had ever encountered behind his simple country-boy exterior. He didn't play the political correctness game, and was very sparing with his praise. A flat out compliment like that had Gerry's heart singing a little, bringing a smile to his face as he hung up.

He half-heartedly started on an after action report, detailing the steps taken to effect the capture, and absent-mindedly pushed his silver glasses back up his nose. Soon, his mind was wandering again, going over the congratulations he'd gotten already, and imagining what else might come. A bunch of the guys had already said they were taking him out for dinner that night, steak, beers, cigars, and maybe a visit after to one of the better strip clubs. That part Marcie didn't need to hear about. A half smile formed on his face when he thought about Jill from the number crunchers in forensic accounting. She'd suggested a more personal celebration when they could get some private time. Gerry had seen her in the gym once, in some kind of leotard or something coming from an aerobics class, and her plain suits in the office were covering up a dynamite body if he was any judge. He hoped he hadn't misread her, but she'd seemed very friendly when she stopped by to congratulate him personally, standing so close and touching his arm and shoulder several times. She'd even found out somewhere about his passion for history, and had gotten him a coffee mug from the Smithsonian Museum of American History. Nothing flashy or anything, a picture of Old Glory in its case in the main gallery, but he'd been thrilled both to get the present and that this sexy woman thought enough about him to know what his interests were.

He ran his fingers through his short brown hair and stretched. Gerry knew he was kind of mousy looking, and that if someone were casting a movie, he'd get the geek role. One of the ongoing annoyances in his life was that people were constantly asking him computer questions, and he didn't know anything about them. Oh sure, he could send an e-mail or search the web, but anything too much more complicated sent him running for the IT guys. Or lately, his daughter. In addition to everything else, Ronnie—no, Veronica—seemed to have a touch with computers, all the more amazing considering she was in middle school. He reached over for his mug and gulped down a nearly room temperature mouthful of coffee. Just as he was making a face at it and wondering if it was worth reheating, his phone rang again. Hurriedly putting the drink down and pushing it beyond easy reach (he knew he'd take another sip without thinking if he got wrapped up in talking to whoever this was, and he did not want anymore of the cooling liquid), he picked up the phone. "Counter-Terrorism, Agent Franklin." He readied himself for another celebratory voice.

After a brief pause, he heard "Agent Gerald Franklin?" The voice was rich, cultured, deep, with a foreign accent.

"Yes, this is he. How can I help you?" Dismissing this as a normal work call, he wondered about cutting out early and walking over to the Mall to look at the Museums, maybe see how the construction was going on that new Indian one.

"This is the man who arrested Fadi Hadad today?"

That got his attention again. "Yes, that was me. Is there something I can help you with?" He wondered if this was someone from the British Embassy, or maybe MI-5.

"You have made a mistake. And I believe you know this." The words sent an surge of fear through Franklin. Some very carefully and resolutely suppressed doubts came surging back on him, and doubt tasted even more sour than the cold coffee in his mouth.

"I have no idea what you're talking about." Franklin tried for the right note of outrage, but sounded more like a whining child to his own ear.

"Agent Franklin. Let us speak as men. Fadi is more child than man. He has poetic dreams of wreaking vengeance upon the Americans, but if you pressed him hard, he more than likely could not even specifically tell you for what. Your information was flawed. The man you called Accountant," Franklin felt mild panic—how did he know that name?— "wished both a generous payout from your agency and some vengeance upon the Hadad family."

"I don't know who you're talking about or what you mean." Franklin's mind raced—some of the evidence had been a bit more vague than he'd let his supervisor think when he made his case for the arrest, but he'd been so sure. *Or maybe you wanted to be sure*, an inner voice echoed in his mind.

"Agent Franklin, I am hoping you are a man of honor. I bring you no deceit. Fadi will no doubt defy you and spout grandiose but vague rhetoric about the honor of Islam, and the Great Satan America, and other such phrases, but he is harmless and largely ignorant. He is no part of any network of operatives, and had the ear of no one of importance. I urge you strongly to re-examine your facts and release him." The voice seemed to almost have a tone of pleading in it now.

"I have no doubt we got the right man." Franklin said, wondering how to get someone's attention to get the call traced. Most of his coworkers, even the omnipresent and annoying Rhonda, seemed to have made themselves scarce.

"We? You've been saying 'I' for this entire conversation until now. Already you show your doubt."

"What is it you want, or believe you know, about this?" Franklin asked. He saw someone walk by the end of the row of cubicles and hurled a pencil at him, only to see it fall far short of its intended target.

"Agent Franklin." there was a pause and a sound almost like a sigh almost at the other end of the line. "This is a family matter. The information you gathered was mostly, although not quite, accurate. You have arrested Fadi for his brother's actions. His brother wishes to make this known to you, and entreat you to review your data."

"So, you're calling for a terrorist about another terrorist?" Some bravado returned to his voice as Franklin looked for something else to throw, only to see the agent walk out of sight.

"Terrorism is largely a matter of perspective, Agent Franklin. What harm would it do to simply review your information, and possibly see that you were deceived by a treacherous, greedy man?" There was another pause. "As we were."

"We? Then you're a terrorist yourself. Why should I listen to a word you say?" Franklin began frantically typing an email to the techs, hoping one of them was paying attention. There was some kind of inter-office messaging system, but he'd never quite managed to make it work right, so he ignored it for now.

"You will not be able to trace this call, Agent. I can hear you typing."

"So you just think I should take you at your word, and send Fadi Hadad on his way with a pat on the head, and say 'Some guy on the phone said it was a mistake'?" Gerald poured scorn into his voice. "I don't think that's gonna happen."

"I think you should recheck your facts. Isn't that what you're supposed to be good at, 'Paperclip'?" The voice sounded emotional now, angry and yet worried somehow.

"Don't call me that you sonovabitch, and unless you have something else to tell me, something useful, we're done here." His badly typed email was sent, and he could only hope they'd get it and be able to work whatever magic they did with servers and routers and magic keyboards for all he knew.

"Please, a moment." There was another pause, as the man on the other end of the line seemed to wrestle his self control back into shape. "I apologize, I know you do not care for the nickname. Do you have family, Agent?"

"I don't see that's any business of yours, and threatening a federal agent isn't a good way to get what you want." Gerry heard his own voice rising to a shriller pitch.

"I am not threatening, I am seeking empathy. Agent Franklin…he is my brother. And he is suffering for my actions. I can not allow this, and I hope you can not either."

Gerry let the thought of his own ne'er-do-well brother Harry float through his head, and wondered if the rehab had worked this time. He'd siphoned off so much of their parents' money already…He shook his head. "What are you suggesting, Mr. Hadad?" He presumed they shared a last name, and was trying to connect with the man he was speaking with, some dimly remembered training about crisis management trying to filter into his consciousness.

"A trade. I will give myself up for my brother's release." There was definitely a note of desperation in the man's voice now. Looking up, Gerry saw his mentor, Jack Conroy, turn the corner of desks and start walking towards him.

"You're a terrorist. We don't negotiate with terrorists. Turn yourself in, and we'll review your brother's case." Gerry wanted to end this, now. This nightmare could not be happening, not on his day of triumph. He couldn't let Jack hear any of this.

There was icy calm in the voice now. "Agent Franklin, if you do not release my brother, I promise you, you will regret it to your dying day. As good as you felt today, as high as you think you will soar from the events of this day, I will tear you down and cast you into the depths."

Gerry tried to think, feeling the pressure of the man's call, his own doubts, the thanks and congratulations he'd gotten, the office he wanted, Jill…He saw Jack almost there and his panic pushed him into making the decision. As his mentor approached, he said "Thank you for calling, but I'm just really not interested in that kind of deal. Have a nice day," and he quickly hung up before he could change his mind.

Jack fixed him with that hard to read stare as he walked up to the desk. "What was that all about?"

Gerry shrugged. "Don't ask me how, but someone got my work number. Trying to get me to switch long distance companies."

Jack looked at him a moment, his face expressionless. "Ok." There was another long pause between student and teacher. "Let's get out of here, kid. You got a dinner coming up, and I want a cigarette. Damn no smoking Nazis." They walked away from the desk, Jack already reaching into his pocket for his pack and lighter.

Far away, a man's face hardened as he put his phone down. He closed his eyes and sent a prayer for forgiveness to Allah. He had tried, and now his brother would pay for his own actions. It was not fair, it was not just, it was another sign of how corrupt the Americans were, for all their lip service to justice. He would learn everything there was to know about this Gerry Franklin. He would find out what he cared about—it certainly wasn't pride in his job. And he would destroy the man utterly. It might take him years, but patience was a virtue, the Europeans were fond of saying. He would be the patient hunter. And Franklin would watch his world go up in flames around him, until he felt the same wrench in his heart that Hadad did now at the thought of Fadi in an American prison. He would have vengeance.

The Present

The Day Before

"And we're on in 3.2.1." The camera man pointed and the large blonde man suddenly seemed a lot more animated and interested than he had a moment ago.

"Thanks, Diane. I tell people this is the greatest job in the world, and days like this are part of why. I'm down here at Nationals Park with star pitcher Hector Valdez. Hector, you're leading the division this year for wins, and your fastball is becoming a legend to the fans, and a curse to the other guy's batters. How do you like the team's chances tomorrow against the Diamondbacks?"

Hector smiled and tried to remember to speak slowly. His accent could still sometimes get the better of him. "We will play our best, of course. And I am sure they will too. But just between us?" He winked at the camera, turning on that roguish smile that was letting him have all manner of success with women in Washington, and caused his manager no end of headaches. "We will beat them."

The sportscaster smiled. "That's the attitude of a winner. What do you think about the people saying you are responsible for turning the team around, and bringing the Nats out of their usual place in the cellar?"

Hector frowned slightly. "I am very good, yes. But I am not playing alone out there. Walker is a great catcher, Simons a fantastic first baseman, and then, we would not be anywhere without Blake at short stop and his streak. I think it is first, him, for RBIs this season in our division? And behind him, Occales? They come to bat and the other team gets scared."

"Well, there you have it, Diane. Even their star pitcher is a team player. There are still some tickets left for tomorrow afternoon's Senator's Day game, so play some hooky, donate to a good cause, and see some of our local lechislators in the special benefit mini-game tomorrow. I'm Bobby Buxton, live at Nationals Park. Back to you Diane." The light on the camera went out and Buxton slumped a bit, somehow looking older and a bit plainer than just a moment ago.

As Diane Harper closed out the newscast from her anchor desk, Wanda Fullbright stormed into the producer's office. "C'mon, Bernie! 'Lechislators'? Is he drunk or just stupid?"

Bernie Holt held up his hands, partially in resignation, partially seeming to ward her off. "I know, Wanda, I know. He can be an idiot. But he knows his sports really well, and the viewers like him." He ran a hand through his hair, making the brown and grey strands stick up in various directions. "What can I do, he's got a contract."

"So do I! And I'm smarter than he is, and everyone here with even half a brain knows that! And I actually know how to pronounce words with more than two syllables." Her last comment was dripping with sarcasm and scorn.

The middle aged producer sighed. "Look, Wanda. You're great, ok? I know that. And someday you'll be at the desk. But right now, I don't have anyplace else for you. So until something opens up, you're traffic and the occasional human interest piece." Her dark brown eyes flared, and her caramel colored skin took on a slight rosy cast.

"And how am I going to get anywhere when I'm mostly doing voice-over off screen, and if I'm really lucky, covering the Boy Scouts Knot Tying championships?" She made a face at that, still convinced that one scout master had been trying to make a pass at her when he demonstrated that knot for the camera by looping the rope around her wrist. Unfortunately for him, she had no interest in rope games.

"I'll try and see what I can do, ok? But right now, it's what I got for you. I promise, I'll try for something more, get you a piece of a bigger story. Diane thinks you're ready, too."

A pleased smile flitted across the woman's face. "She does? She told you that?"

He nodded, glad he'd held this news in reserve for when he needed it, like now. "Yeah, she thinks you're great, like the rest of us. Just give it some time, ok?"

The reluctant traffic reporter finally nodded. "Ok. Just...he's such an IDIOT." She then flashed the smile that had won her several beauty pageants when she was in college. "But, he'll screw himself up soon. He's too dumb not too." She left the office, and Bernie heaved a sigh of relief. He could handle the demands of putting together the best news show in the nation's capital, but juggling some of these on air personalities was starting to get the better of him. He pulled an antacid from the roll in his desk drawer and chewed it. She was right, though. Buxton was an idiot.

In a conference room in one of the buildings belonging to the Washington Metropolitan Police Department, Field Training Officer Raphael Segovia turned away from the television with a questioning look on his face. "Lechislators?"

His most recent graduate from trainee to full police officer shrugged. "I guess that's like a horny politician. Isn't that most of them, though?" Farris Fakhoury shook his head at the man's obvious idiocy.

The pair had met up in an unused room to go over Fakhoury's patrol that day. While he was released from the field training program, he still valued the guidance and advice of his former teacher. "So, follow up on the stolen car later, make sure your notes are ready if it goes to court, and...anything else?"

Farris smiled. "Rafe's Rule #4—know when it's time to go home. Or at least away from here."

"Yeah, fair enough. What you up to tonight?" The older man looked over at the eager young rookie.

"Nothing really. Quiet night at home, I guess." Farris gathered up his notebook and got to his feet.

"Having some problems on the shift?" Rafe asked, watching him.

"Yeah, well…I'm an Arab, and a Muslim, and I don't hide either one, so I get a lot of crap about being a terrorist, or working for them, or whatever. They'll figure it out eventually. Or not. Hey, I'm still a cop. That's what I wanted to be. If they're too dumb to see it, that's not my problem."

Rafe nodded. "Still sounds lonely. You know how to get hold of me if there's anything you need," he said.

"I'm fine. I just need to make some friends somewhere. And maybe get out a little more." Farris shook hands with the older man and left, walking down to the elevator.

A passing officer greeted him with "Hey, Osama."

"Good night, asshole," he said in a calm tone that threw the other man off.

"What did you call me?" the officer asked, his face flushing with anger as the doors opened.

"Better run by the clinic and get your hearing checked. I hear that goes when you get old." Farris waved at the older man and was amused by his shocked look as the doors closed.

"Who's that punk ass kid think he is?" the veteran fumed, staring at the closed doors.

"Probably someone who doesn't need to take racist crap from someone he's supposed to be working with, LaSalle."

Turning, he saw Rafe walking down the hallway. "Did you hear what he called me?"

"Yeah. Heard what you called him, too. Lay off the kid, LaSalle. He's good. And he don't need your crap."

"What're you, a terrorist spokesman now?" LaSalle's face took on an expression of cruel amusement.

"No, I'm his FTO. And his friend. And I got seniority on you. And I know Cooper in IA, and you're starting to sound like you have some racial issues that might need looking into." Rafe stared the man down. "You really wanna keep going with this? I could have a word with your captain, suggest you take some of those cultural diversity classes. Those are always fun."

LaSalle turned away, mumbling something about "rat lover," but Rafe was satisfied for now.

Outside, Farris decided he'd walk to his destination to clear his head. He did his best to not let things like that bother him, but sometimes...he shook his head sadly. America touted itself as the melting pot, but there was an ugly current of racism and fear just under the surface in a lot of places. And since the September 11 attacks, it wasn't a good time to be either Arabic or Muslim in the US. Some people were fine, but the paranoids, racists, and bullies were having a field day with his people, most of whom thought the attacks were abominable crimes against all people everywhere. He tried to shake himself out of it as he approached the mosque and prepared himself for evening prayer.

Ariel Hanson sat at her desk, poring over some intel reports. The problem with hunting terrorists wasn't that there were no leads or tips, it was that there were too many. People scared of their neighbors, people with a grudge, schizophrenics who were convinced they had special knowledge, paranoids who believed themselves targets, and even well meaning, fairly well adjusted people who misunderstood something provided a never ending stream of useless confusion, but it all needed to be followed up on. The Department of Homeland Security was a fledgling organization by government standards, and there was still a lot of "make it up as you go along" because no one had any real experience at such a mammoth undertaking. So many different agencies had been combined under the DHS umbrella, Immigration and Customs Enforcement, the Coast Guard, Secret Service, and the Transportation Security Administration, to name just a few, that there was still massive reorganizing going on, years after they were shoved together. Each agency had its own way of doing things, its own people, and its own general preferences and prejudices, and they were still all being smoothed out. There were bumps in the road, gaps in the information distribution, and old inter-agency rivalries still surfacing from time to time, even though they were all on the same side...in theory, anyway.

Ariel had been with DHS for a few years now, and had gradually convinced her superiors that she had some valid ideas about how to change things. Her background in library science and information technology made for an unlikely resume in the DHS, but she was meeting with a good many successes and starting to make a name for herself. She had begun analyzing how information in the organization was shared, or not in some cases. Once, when trying to explain yet again what she did at a party she'd made the mistake of going to, she'd summarized her job by saying "Ok, you've heard of the information super highway? I'm a traffic cop. I keep it moving, make sure the roads aren't blocked, and clear up jams." She'd watched the man's eyes start to glaze over, and dismissed him in her mind at that point.

Her cubicle walls were covered with not only pictures of terrorists, reports of locations, maps, theoretical organizational charts of terrorist groups and alliances, but also financial tracking sheets and even records of informants (names coded, of course), which ones were somewhat reliable, which were nut jobs of whatever stripe, and which they just weren't sure of. She'd weeded out some that were thought to be good sources by showing that they were mostly shopping the same stories around to the different agencies, and that they weren't actually telling them anything new. Ariel also made a point to cultivate contacts in different agencies, both within and outside of DHS. She'd befriended a computer geek at the Pentagon logistics office, administrative assistants in the IRS and US Marshals, agents with the Secret Service, and a few DEA guys along the way, among others. She was always the same: "What do you know, what do you have for me? Good story? Rumor? Anything about (insert whatever she was looking into at that point)?" On the other hand, she also made damn sure these people got good tips when she came across them, and information went to the people who actually needed it. A lot of her work had been claimed by other people along the way, but she was fine with that. She knew what she did mattered, and a growing number valued her skills and her incredible mind. She wasn't above using other means to get what she needed either. Ariel was 5'7" with waist-length blonde hair, and a body toned by a combination of running, kick boxing, and rock climbing. She didn't sleep around, and she made that clear, but her looks and Southern charm, when she turned it on, got her better results than any memo, and she knew it.

"Hey, catch Osama yet?" Jeff Burkely wandered into her cubicle, bearing a coffee cup from Starbucks and a muffin of some kind.

Her eyes locked in on the food and drink, and she heard her stomach rumble. She'd had lunch…hadn't she? She wasn't sure suddenly. His smile seemed to indicate Jeff had heard her stomach, so she gave up any pretense at focusing on her work and said, "No. Gimme!"

He laughed and passed over the snack. "You skipped lunch. Again." Ariel had never really been able to figure Jeff out. He hadn't hit on her, wasn't gay, didn't seem to be looking for help with his own projects, just one day had said something or other nice about some work she'd been doing and they had slowly become friends, sort of. They didn't spend time together away from work, hadn't gone to lunch (she had enough rumor to deal with in that department), and didn't share hobbies. But somehow, they'd grown close, and he'd become one of the few who could tease her about her work without her getting either mad or defensive. He moved one of her many notebooks—"Binder Queen" was one of her nicknames she knew—and sat down in the other chair, sipping his own coffee.

"Anything new on the border?" she asked around a mouth full of banana walnut muffin.

"Ah, some wanna be drug king was setting up surveillance on one of the check points in New Mexico, telephoto cameras and mics and all that. Called a buddy of mine in the Air Force, who made a few calls, and one of those drones buzzed the guy. From what they said, he's probably still running." Jeff laughed. "It wasn't even armed. Moron." as he shook his head at the memory.

She sipped her coffee and then rubbed her eyes. Maybe she was spending too much time with computer monitors and print outs. He saw the movement and she held up a finger before he could say anything. "Hey, I'm going climbing next weekend, I've got a date tomorrow night, and I'm eating ok." She looked down at the remains of the muffin. "Mostly. And what about you? Have you managed to say more than three words in a row to Angela?" Normally fairly self confident, Jeff had managed to get himself hung up completely on a woman he met at one of the local bars, and the best he had managed was a few excruciatingly tongue-tied conversations that left him calling himself all manner of names afterwards. He shook his head and decided to change the subject.

"Well now that we've finished that bit, I've got something for you." Jeff pulled a folded piece of paper out of his pocket.

"What, more than muffins and coffee?"

"Yeah, better. I think. I'm actually not sure." Jeff worked

with several different border agencies as a coordinator, a smaller scale version of what Ariel was trying to set up with all the agencies. "One of my guys picked up a coyote, but he wasn't running immigrants this time." Ariel knew that coyotes specialized in smuggling illegals across the border from Mexico into the US, but often as not abandoned their charges in the desert and took their money.

"Drugs?" It was a likely second guess; many of them side lined in the narcotics trade.

"Well, they started with that, and he wanted to cut a deal. So he started telling this story about this really weird guy who paid him extra to take just him across. Said the guy scared the hell out of him, and he thought he was going to end up shot in the head. Now here's where it gets interesting. He said the guy was about six foot tall, an Arab…and dressed all in grey."

Ariel's head shot up. "Nazzir?"

Jeff shrugged. "Sounds like it. I know he's one of your special interests, figured you'd want to know."

Ariel had long ago run across rumor of a man who used the name Nazzir. He was supposed to be an amazingly skilled terrorist, proficient with all manner of weapons and explosives, and was praised as some kind of second coming of Saladin in some circles. He seemed to be able to cross borders easily, and hit a bewildering array of targets all around the world. The more she'd dug into his story, the more Ariel was intrigued. He wasn't affiliated with any one group, he usually worked alone, and he didn't seem to have any one particular ideological ax to grind. In fact, she thought he was mostly a mercenary. He didn't do big dramatic statements, and some of the killing attributed to him seemed more like murder for hire than striking back against the infidels of America, or whatever phrase you cared to pick.

She pulled the paper from his non-resisting hand and scanned it rapidly. One of Nazzir's trademarks was his penchant for dressing in shades of grey, and the description tallied with the vague reports she'd managed to put together over several months of what he supposedly looked like. "I think you have something here." She glanced over at the clock quickly, running ideas through her head.

"Go. Call him. Work that weird magic of yours and go get this guy." He stood up and wandered back to his own desk, giving her a wave while walking away as she thanked him.

Ariel picked up her phone and hit speed dial. After two rings, she heard, "Holmes."

"Wow, not even saying 'How may I help you' or anything anymore? What about customer satisfaction?" Ariel teased a bit.

"Caller ID, Ariel. I was pretty sure it was you. What's up?"

"I think we should have lunch." She carefully placed the emphasis on the last word.

"Hmm. Little late, but I'm guessing you forgot to eat again. Chen's?" His deep voice rumbled down the line.

"Sure. See you in thirty?" After they both agreed to meet, she logged off her computer, scooped up her purse, and headed out, telling the admin out front she had a meeting.

Soon, she walked into an upscale Chinese restaurant and declined the greeter's offer to seat her. Looking around, she saw a tall, well-dressed black man sitting at the back corner table, reading the sports page of the Post. Ariel walked over, and as she reached for the chair he said, "This Valdez guy, what do you think? He's got some ego on him, but he seems like he's turning the team around." He paused, eyes skimming the newspaper again. "Though I'll give him credit, seems like he's trying to ramp that down some, the ego."

She made a face. "You know I don't follow baseball." A waiter approached, took their orders, and quickly departed. Holmes put down the paper and looked over at her.

"Not that I don't enjoy your company, but what do you

have?"

Ariel had been meeting with Mark Holmes for months now. They had crossed paths at a conference on information technology for the government, and he'd surprised her by knowing who she was, and saying he liked what he'd heard about her work. They had lunch that day, and had continued doing it fairly regularly. Aside from getting on well, they had both realized the benefits of sharing information, and did so often. While rumors had floated around about the two, they both ignored them, and by meeting on their own time, managed to share more than either felt they could at the office. There was still some rivalry between FBI, where Holmes worked, and DHS, whatever the official party line was, and neither of them had the patience for it.

Wordlessly, she produced the copy of Jeff's page of notes that she'd stopped to make on the way out of the office from her purse and slid it over to him. His dark eyes scanned the paper quickly, and his eyebrows rose a bit. "Nazzir? That's not good."

"Why not? I thought you wanted to get him as bad as I do?" Ariel looked over at him, a bit puzzled.

"Because I was going to call you tomorrow and suggest lunch. I'm hearing bits and pieces of something that sounds big, but no one seems to know what's going on. The pieces don't seem to fit. And now this guy coming in…he's never good news." Holmes frowned again. "I don't like it. And this was a few days ago, God only knows where he is by now."

The two shared thoughts, theories, and rumors over orange chicken and sesame beef, and eventually headed back to their respective offices, each feeling something was in the air, but not being able to quite put a name to it. Once back at the FBI Counter-Terrorism offices, Mark went to his desk. Inside his office, he closed the door and carefully took off his jacket, placing it up on a hanger he'd put on the door for just that reason. One of Holmes' few indulgences was being a clothes horse, and he liked to take good care of his suits. Finding no new messages on either his voice mail or computer, he began making a few calls to see if he could find anyone who had heard anything that would help him work out what in the hell was going on.

A floor above in a much larger office, Gerry Franklin sweated. He'd been having a bad day and things kept getting worse. Were he the type to count his blessings, he would have realized how much fortune had favored him. His large office was only the start of it. His daughter Veronica had picked up several scholarships and was now trying to choose between them, and which college she'd go to on early admission. His years-long affair with Jill Fowler had been even better than he'd imagined. Not only was she amazing in bed, but her gift with numbers allowed her a near perfect record with playing the stock market, and he'd benefitted from several of her tips over the years. And his reputation in the office had grown, largely due to his persistence. He wasn't the most brilliant investigator or the world's most creative thinker, but he was a master of detail, and words used to describe his work on cases were often ones like "stubborn," "dogged," or "relentless." He kind of liked the last one, although he carefully pretended not to know what people said about him.

He and Marcie had been fighting again lately, which made it even more unlikely she'd let them stop seeing this pain in the ass marriage counselor. He was a great provider, remembered birthdays and their anniversary, didn't bitch about her mom coming to town (far too often he privately thought) and thought she had a pretty good deal going. They'd had a particularly bad fight last night after she'd accused him of not listening when she was going on and on about some special field trip or something with Veronica this week. He'd been running the numbers on the stock portfolio, and seeing that once again Jill had steered him right, which led him into various memories about her of the kind he really couldn't share with his wife, so didn't have a good answer ready for the "Well what ARE you thinking about then?" she had fired at him. He'd been having trouble concentrating all day, and was wondering if he could come up with an excuse to visit Jill's office. They kept their work contact strictly professional, even cool. Some of their co-workers thought they actually didn't like each other. But maybe he could come up with some kind of follow-the-money type question. He half heartedly tried to sort through the sea of paper that seemed to have materialized on his desk since he'd gone to lunch earlier with one of the Assistant Directors in his branch, who had dropped maddeningly vague hints about Gerry maybe getting a promotion soon. Or maybe not. He'd had trouble following what the man said, and the scotch hadn't helped, nor had AD Grant's penchant for speaking in bureaucratese with a healthy helping of allusions. He ran his fingers through his hair as he stared at another document that didn't tell him anything he wanted to know right now. He let his eyes roam the walls and take in the various photos of him shaking hands with politicians, at press conferences, and at one of the re-opening parties for the American History Museum after it closed for a long-delayed and much needed remodeling. Those with an eye for such things would note very few appearances by either Marcie or Veronica on that wall.

Suddenly, his phone rang. He glared at it, noting it was his secretary Jennie's extension. With an exaggerated sigh, he punched the speaker button, shuffling some papers with his other hand to make himself sound busy. "Yes, Jennie?"

"I hate to disturb you, Mr. Franklin, but I have a Sheriff Alex Doyle on the line? From Arizona? He said he had a confidential matter to discuss with you?" Jennie was a good assistant, but her habit of making everything sound like a question when she was nervous truly grated on him. It was a bad enough habit with the twenty-something women he'd hear sometimes on the Metro or in bars or restaurants, but coming from a woman in her 40s, it just plain sounded ridiculous.

He firmly bit down on his first response, which was asking her if she was sure. She wouldn't get it, and never really believed it when anyone told her about her questioning voice. "All right, Jennie, put him through."

There was a clicking and then "Hello?" The voice carried a slight accent that reminded Franklin of his mentor, Conroy. His eyes went to the picture from Conroy's retirement dinner last year. They kept in touch occasionally, and although Gerry would never admit it, he missed the older man's advice and quiet steadiness.

"Good afternoon Sheriff, this is Special Agent Franklin. How may I help you?"

"Agent Franklin, I'm a simple man, and I have to account to the budget folks about these long distance calls, so let me cut right to the chase here. You're Gerald Franklin, right?"

The agent looked at the phone, irritation on his face. "Yes, that's my name. Did you have a question about terrorism I could help you with?" Occasionally, his name got out to the various small law enforcement agencies, and he got calls with random seeming questions. He could usually fob the caller off on someone else and get back to work quickly enough.

"You got a brother name of Harry Milhouse Franklin?" Gerry's stomach lurched and he reached automatically for his antacids.

"Yes, Sheriff Doyle, I do." He didn't bother to keep the weariness from his voice. "What'd he do now? Drugs again?" His damn brother had never managed to get his life together despite repeated promises and trips to various drug treatment programs. Their father had cut him off, causing a rare fight between him and his wife. Eventually she sadly had agreed after Harry's quick trip home following yet another cure-all program had resulted in several fights about his plans for the future and the theft of a hundred dollars or so from her purse.

"Well, I'm afraid it ain't that simple, Agent. Looks like he got himself high as a kite and had a kinda disagreement you could say with his dealer."

Gerry felt a major tension headache spreading between his temples now as his neck stiffened. "How bad is it, Sheriff?"

"Well, it's pretty bad. The dealer's dead, the knife has your brother's prints all over it, and he's got blood all over his clothes. Says he don't remember any of it. I guess this call is by way of a professional courtesy. The prosecutor is talking it over with his assistant there, but I do believe they're gonna charge the boy with Murder Two." Gerry barely managed to not swear into the phone.

"That's crazy. He's got a nasty drug problem, but he hasn't even been in a fight since he was in fifth grade." Even as he heard himself say the words, he recognized the sound of his voice—just like that of any number of criminals' families over the years, all sure that whatever the evidence said, their little boy, girl, sister, brother, whatever, couldn't possibly be mixed up in something like this.

It quickly became apparent the sheriff knew the tone as well. "I know it's hard to hear something like this, Agent. We got him in protective custody, so he's not with other prisoners or anything. If y'all want to give me a number, I can fax out a list of some of the better local lawyers, unless you got one you want to send or something."

"I...no, we don't have one...Sheriff, I'm going to put you with my admin, Jennie, she can give you the fax number and get your office information. Thanks for the call." Gerry had no idea what to do now, he wasn't used to being on this side of things. Damn Harry anyway! Was it so much to ask that he get his shit together and finally start acting like a grown-up?

And now he'd finally snapped and killed someone? How in hell was he going to make this call to Mom and Dad? He transferred the sheriff back to Jennie and tried to think. As soon as he saw she was off the phone, he buzzed the intercom to her and said "I'm not taking any calls from press today, Jennie."

He disconnected after hearing her condolences and sat at his desk, his eyes going blank. He nearly snarled when the knock came at his door, but he mastered himself barely and said, "Come in."

The door opened to reveal Lisa Carter, the office's current intern. Most college students wouldn't be able to get an internship at such a prestigious place, but her grandfather was a Congressman with a good bit of pull, and no one really wanted to get on his bad side. "I finished that sorting project, Agent Franklin, and got all the boxes labeled. Is there something else." her voice trailed off a bit as she got a better look at him. "Are you all right? Should I get you some coffee or something?" More to get her back out of the office than because he wanted any, he agreed. He'd have to come up with another project for her, and couldn't keep handing her boring scut work. She'd complain to grandpa, and then the higher ups would be on him for creating bad blood with the Congressman who sat on several Justice Department Committees, especially the all-important budgetary group.

As she left, he saw Agent Ron Craigson waiting by Jennie's desk and groaned. The man had graduated from the Academy a few months ago, gotten assigned to his office on some luck of the draw kind of lottery, and his persistent cheer and eagerness was wearing on the older agent. What did he want now? Another memo on how to reorganize the files? Some kind of new computer toy that would make everything faster? Or more on that inter-office group that Hanson woman was trying to form?

Franklin's ruminations were cut short when his cell phone

buzzed in his shirt pocket. His irritation faded when he saw the name of his old mentor. He flipped the phone open and said "Boy, I could use a friendly voice about now. You would not believe the day I'm having." He winced a bit as he said it. His lowering of his habitual guard with his old mentor made his voice sound like it was whining to him, something he hated.

He nearly dropped the phone when he heard the voice—cold, computer modulated, nothing like Conroy's simple, country boy tones. "Agent Franklin. Several years ago, a promise was made to you that you would come to regret your actions that led to the arrest, imprisonment, and later death of a man you knew to be innocent and your refusal to even admit to the error you made. Your debt is coming due. Former Agent Conroy has paid part of it. Your sins will fall on those you love."

"What? Who is this? Jack, this isn't funny." Gerry tried to keep his voice sounding professional.

"You know of what I speak. Remember your 'big break' that made your fortune for you in your career. You will see what price your arrogance." The caller disconnected. Gerry felt a surge of fear as carefully repressed memories leapt to the surface of his brain, doubts he pretended so hard didn't exist he'd almost convinced himself they weren't real boiled up into his consciousness, and years of careful denial fell apart. He tried to call Jack back, several times, and kept getting no answer, just his maddeningly laconic "I'm busy, leave a message or call back."

Moving fast, he got up and half walked, half staggered to the door, just as Lisa came back with the coffee. He took it from her quickly, barely knowing what he was doing or saying. "Agent Craigson, get the address for retired agent Jack Conroy, and go check on him. Now. Top priority."

The agent practically leapt out of the chair he'd been sitting in. "Sir? Shouldn't we call the local police if we suspect a problem with…"

Gerry cut him off. "No. This has some…security considerations. Go, quickly, and tell me what you find."

Lisa blinked at this exchange, seeing her usually composed boss so shaken. "Sir, is there something else I should…"

He couldn't take her questions or up-beat manner or anything else right now. "Go with him. Ask him questions. Learn something. When you find out he's ok, you can have dinner or something. Now get going!" He closed the door forcefully, just short of a slam. The two looked at each other, both uncertain, but decided they'd best get going. They left the outer office just as Jennie was coming back to her desk.

Lisa got out a hurried "Sorry, Mrs. Doorfner, I have to go run an errand," before she and Craigson went down the hall to the elevators quickly and talking animatedly. Jennie sniffed her disapproval. She'd thought that young Craigson had been spending too much time here to try and ingratiate himself with Agent Franklin (even in her head, she stuck to the man's formal title), but maybe he'd been working up the nerve to ask Lisa out. These young people had no sense of propriety these days. She sat down and opened her desk drawer, pulling out her Bible to find a passage to inspire her properly to send up a prayer on behalf of her beleaguered employer, surrounded by such flighty youngsters when he clearly needed all the support he could get in this trying time. That nice sheriff had outlined the nature of his call while getting the fax number and leaving all his information with her. Poor Agent Franklin was surely being tested today.

While Agent Craigson and Intern Carter signed out a car and picked up a file about Conroy, and Gerry searched his desk for something for his now amazingly powerful headache, Hector Valdez smiled at Gina Wright. The young woman had been part of the camera crew who had filmed the spot with "Bucky" as he preferred to be called, and caught the pitcher's attention. "So, I have some time before I need to be back before the game. Would you like to get some dinner?" As the camerawoman agreed, figuring if nothing else she'd have a great story for next girl's night out, Ariel Hanson frowned at her computer screen. Holmes had forwarded to her the various bits and pieces of rumor he'd been hearing, and it really wasn't making a lot of sense. There were stories about a truck hijacking planned, or a series of them, but nothing definite. Some said that armored cars were going to be used to run over as many people as possible on the way to ram public buildings, some said tanker trucks were going to be overturned to cause accidents and tie up traffic, although to her that sounded more like annoyance than terrorism. She wondered briefly if a not-quite-as-committed terrorist would be something like an annoyance-ist. Oh well, sounded better than "lechislator." She made a few calls, not so much trying to get information but more in the, "Hey, if you hear anything weird going on the next few days, call me" vein. There was just no pattern she could put her finger on with all these tips and rumors and facts and bits of fact. A few suspected terrorists were thought to be on the move toward the East Coast, but whether to New York City, Washington, or someplace else was different from story to story. Bombings, shootings, robberies to fund other activities, all manner of things were swirling around out there. She was pretty sure something was in the works, and that it would be ugly, but what it was, or when, or where...well, those were the questions, weren't they? Muttering to herself, she went back to sifting reports and whispers and rumors and tried to think like a terrorist. What would she do with these bits and pieces?

Elsewhere, Jill Fowler got home a bit early for once. She'd taken a half day at work and gone to her gym to get in a work out. She was great looking for her age, and knew it, but also knew it would take a lot of hard work to stay that way. In her upper forties, she had a body many twenty year olds admired. So far, she'd managed to avoid resorting to any plastic surgery. She'd been given a good figure to start with, and worked at keeping it. Today had been aerobic kick boxing followed by weight machines followed by half an hour on the treadmill. She unlocked the door to her apartment and stepped in, dropping her bag with her work clothes in it by the door. She'd come straight home, planning on showering and changing here, and was still in her spandex workout clothes. Besides, she'd turned a few heads on the way in, and that was always a rush.

She moved into the living room and placed her laptop case on the couch. After the shower and a quick dinner, she would go back to work, making up the time she took off earlier, poring over more records of various accounts that were held suspect by various other agents. She also pondered digging some more into her special project. She had to be careful to not raise alarms until she was sure. Jill took a great pride in her ability to find patterns others missed, and her skill with numbers. Of course, her other accomplishments were what kept Gerry coming back to her. Occasionally, she pondered breaking things off with him, but they were both having fun, and his marriage was seriously rocky long before she approached him. She'd met Marcie a few times at office parties, and didn't see the attraction, or why she stayed with him. Marcie Franklin seemed like an intelligent woman and clearly had some sense of style from her clothing and make up. What in the world was she doing with Gerry? Sleeping with him on occasion was one thing, and he'd gotten much better with what she liked to think was her expert tutelage. But living with him all the time, raising a child? She shook her head and shrugged. Took all kinds, she guessed.

She turned towards her bedroom and the shower she'd been looking forward to, reaching up to start sliding the straps down her shoulders from her top when she felt the sick bite of fear as a man emerged from behind her door with a pistol pointed at her. "Agent Fowler, do nothing foolish and you will not be harmed." His voice was accented, and he looked Arabic. He was wearing a nice quality grey suit, a piece of her brain noted as she stood there, frozen. His eyes ran over her, but it seemed more like a professional assessment than any kind of leering. "I can't imagine you have your weapon on you in that outfit—where would you put it? Tell me where it is."

She stood mute for a moment and he took a half step closer. "I do not need to hurt you, but I will not take any risks I do not need to. Cooperate with me, Agent. It is in your best interests."

"My bag, in the hall." her voice broke. God, what was he doing here? How did he get in? Why had she been stupid enough not to at least clip on her mace?

"Very good. That was not so hard, was it? See, reason may yet prevail here, if you do nothing foolish. Now tell me, Jill Fowler of the FBI, are you expecting company tonight? Think carefully before you answer. If we are unexpectedly interrupted, I will of course have to kill whoever it is that arrives." He knew her name, too. Biting her lower lip, she shook her head and tried to think of a plan. Her gun was too far away, there was no hope there. "If you will pardon the observation, I can see why Agent Franklin is attracted. You keep yourself very fit, certainly."

She wished she were wearing more, suddenly. Her outfit was great for the gym, but left little to the imagination and she felt very exposed and vulnerable. She put one hand up to her chest, reflexively, not thinking about it. "No…no one's coming by."

"I believe you. And hope you speak truth for their sake." The man dipped his hand in his pocket for something, came up with what looked like a black pistol, pointed it at her and fired. She felt a stab as her whole body lit up in pain and she passed out.

Time passed, more pleasantly for some than others. Jill Fowler was unconscious, and didn't feel it when she was carried to her bedroom and dropped unceremoniously onto her bed. Harry Franklin cowered in his jail cell, his fogged brain trying to work out whether or not he'd actually killed someone. Hector Valdez told Gina Wright, "You know, I need to go to bed early the night before a game," and turned on his winning smile, and she thought, "Oh, what the hell, should be fun." Ariel Hanson was distracted during her kick boxing class and lost her sparring match badly, annoyance adding itself to her list of woes. Marcie Franklin closed up her real estate office and went home, thinking about what to make for her and Veronica's dinner and wondering when Gerry would finally get around to coming home, or at least calling to say he'd be late. Prayers long over, Officer Farris Fakhoury moved through a work out at his gym, temporarily distracted by the cute blonde who walked out of the kick boxing class looking great as always but really annoyed. "Bucky" Buxton was drowning his sorrows at his favorite sports bar, eyeing one of the bats hung on the wall and wondering if he'd need to pick it up and start swinging the next time someone made a "lechislator" joke. For Christ's sake, he'd made a simple slip of the tongue.

Finally, after a few wrong turnings despite directions and a GPS, Agent Craigson pulled the car into a rural driveway. Conroy had chosen a very secluded spot in the mountains of the western part of Virginia to retire in, and it had taken them some time to get here. Craigson was a bit nervous about having Lisa Carter along for several reasons. While there was probably nothing wrong out here, she was still a civilian, and he didn't understand why Supervisory Agent Franklin had detailed her to come with him. Plus, she was related to an important Congressman, and he was very aware of that. And finally, for all his Academy training and time in Washington,

Craigson had been mostly raised in rural Alabama, and wasn't really comfortable with a young, attractive white woman being alone in the car with him. He kept almost expecting some of the rednecks who'd taunted him in his youth to step from the shadows and slur out "Whatchoo doin' with a white girl, boy?" Maybe just being out in the sticks here was bringing back bad memories for him. He shut off the engine and undid his seatbelt, turning to her. "Miss Carter." he began.

"Lisa, please." She smiled at him.

"Lisa then. I need you to stay here for me. I'll just go take a quick look, ring the bell," he looked at the rustic cabin again, "if there is one anyway, and see if Agent Conroy is ok."

She sighed, but leaned back in the seat. Truthfully, she didn't really want to be way out here in the middle of nowhere. She'd asked for this internship to help make up her mind about law school as a way to become an FBI Agent. She'd decided that she liked the idea, but so far Agent Franklin hadn't impressed her at all. He seemed like kind of a jerk, really, although of course she'd never say that. Her momma always told her not to say anything if she couldn't say anything nice. Oh well, at least she'd been sent out here with a cute agent and not that Bible thumping secretary that guarded Franklin's office door like a dragon with overly minted breath instead of fire. She was pretty sure that Jennie kept slipping away from her desk to sneak cigarettes and was hiding it from everyone.

Bored, she watched as Craigson went up the simple flagstone walk to the door. She saw him start to knock, then lower his hand and simply push the door open. The change was dramatic—he crouched down, drew his pistol, and became much more intent, focused. He moved inside and she pulled her out her cell phone. If this was a horror movie, she thought, it'd be dead. The battery was fine, and while it wasn't a great signal, there was some. She punched in 9-1 and waited, checking the address again on the paperwork. If something went bad, she wanted to know exactly where to tell the cavalry to come.

A few moments later, she saw Craigson speed out the door, and she nearly hit the final "1" with her posed thumb. He stumbled down the path, and she tried to see both if he was hurt and if someone was chasing him. He got halfway down the walk and bent over sharply at the waist. At first, she thought he was passing out, and then she realized he was throwing up. She'd had enough. Closing her cell phone, she got out of the car and moved towards him. "Agent Craigson? Are you ok?"

He waved her back with his arm, still bent over. His dark complexion, or what she could see of it in the rapidly dying sunset, looked gray. He tried to breathe in again, and she moved back to the car, getting a bottle of water out of the back seat. "Here, rinse your mouth out. Are you ok?"

He sipped, swirled the water, and spat, and looked up at her weakly. "Thanks. Don't go in there."

She looked over his shoulder at the doorway. "I'm guessing Agent Conroy *isn't* ok?"

He shook his head. "He's dead. He died ugly." He closed his eyes and straightened up. "I think someone was working on him with a knife. I need to call this in."

She nodded and moved past him.

"You really don't want to go in there. And don't touch anything!" Craigson yelled as he pulled his phone out, then muttered "Where the hell are we?"

"5704 Ridgeline Terrace," she supplied, peering inside. It was, as he'd said, an ugly sight. The man was strapped to a chair, and there was blood everywhere. He'd bled a long time from many cuts, made to hurt and cause pain, not kill. She shivered a bit and moved back, returning to Craigson and waiting as he made the call, identified himself, and requested medics and coroners. Before he called Franklin, he looked over at her.

"So…you're ok?" His voice was still a little shaky, but better.

"My daddy was a hunter. He took me when me and my brother Billy were real young. I've seen worse than that, but not in a long time. Someone wanted him to suffer, or tell them something, or both." She looked back at the agent, who nodded in agreement.

"Yeah, that wasn't just a killing. That was something more. I just…wasn't expecting it, you know?" His voice had a slight pleading note, and she knew what he was asking, and wouldn't make him say it.

"I won't tell. I felt like doing the same thing, I just didn't want you to think I was having 'the vapors' " she said and hugely magnified her Southern accent on the last two words. He managed a short bark of laughter.

"You sound like my gramma." he said as he dialed Franklin's office line, and got voice mail. He left a terse, call me ASAP type message and then pulled Franklin's card out of his wallet to find the cell phone number. Another card came part way out, and he remembered meeting another agent who was always looking out for strange things, especially lately. Craigson thought that after he finally contacted Franklin, or at least left all the message he could, that Agent Holmes might be due a call as well.

As Craigson tried to find Franklin without success, and a sleepy rural sheriff's office had a brutal murder/torture dropped in their laps, and a special FBI team began moving out for 5704 Ridgeline Terrace, a man who had used many names strolled along the bank of the Potomac, watching the twilight deepen. Aesthetically, he liked Washington, DC. There was a grandeur about the buildings that he could appreciate. He'd read up on most of the more impressive buildings, and many of the men who had inspired the various monuments. He wondered what Jefferson would have thought of the world situation these days. He admired some of what he'd read of the man, and found it curious that such a genius and proponent of liberty never quite saw the irony of his owning slaves, even fathering children with one of them, it appeared. The man slowly walked back up the marble steps from the river to the level of the National Mall and looked around at the buildings in the distance. Washington, DC, had a certain beauty to it, he supposed. He wondered what it would look like by this time tomorrow.

The Day Of

Early Morning

At roughly two in the morning, a no longer fresh and bright Agent Craigson and Intern Carter were finally released from the scene, after answering variations of the same questions over and over again, for the local police, the investigating FBI team, the Internal Affairs unit, and even a coroner who had apparently watched too much CSI and thought he was an actual investigator. No, neither of them knew former Agent Conroy personally. Yes, they were sent here by Supervisory Agent Franklin. No, he didn't say why he was sending them. Yes, it was unusual to send a civilian intern on such a matter. No, they hadn't been able to reach Agent Franklin's cell phone. No, they didn't have his home number, and would prefer someone else make the decision to call him at home at this hour (as the evening progressed). Yes, they'd both gone inside. No, they hadn't touched anything.

Climbing wearily back into the car, Craigson looked over at Carter. "Thanks, for saying that. You didn't have to do that."

She made a dismissive motion with her hand. "I'm here a few months, then I leave. I may or may not try for a job here down the road. What do I care if they think I threw up by the pathway after seeing inside?"

"Still...appreciate it." he answered as he fished his cell out of his pocket.

"If you really appreciate it, just don't fall asleep on the

drive back." She yawned hugely. "Who are you calling?"

"Know a guy who wanted to be kept informed about strange things happening. I think this counts." Craigson dialed the number on the card he'd been given and left a somewhat detailed message on Holmes' cell. "Gonna stop for coffee once I see something that looks like civilization again. You want anything?" They debated coffee types and flavors and additives for a while, which kept them awake long enough to find a small diner that was miraculously still open. A few minutes later, Craigson drove on into the night, feeling at the very least properly caffeinated finally.

Gerry Franklin thrashed awake from a confused nightmare where everyone was laughing at him, saying all his cases had been luck or mistakes, pointing fingers at him, and taunting cries of "Paperclip is an idiot, a fool, just lucky." The phone rang again, as he struggled blearily to reach for it on the night stand and picked it up finally. "Franklin." he rasped out.

"Agent Franklin." The digitized voice in his ear was better than a gallon of diner coffee for clearing the agent's head suddenly. "I had hoped to not disturb your family, but you don't seem to be answering your cell phone."

"What….what do you want?" He blinked, trying to figure out who this could be and why they were harassing him.

"You do, I am sure, have caller ID. Check the number, and come look for yourself. Or send another poor unsuspecting agent like before."

"What? What happened to Craigson?" Franklin demanded of what he realized was a dead line. He, or she, had hung up. He looked at the calls log after hitting the wrong button twice with sleep fogged reflexes. FOWLER, JILL came up.

"Oh, shit." he muttered as he quickly got up and started finding clothes.

"Whaizzit?" Marcie murmured from her side of the bed.

"Work problem, hon. Gotta go." He hurriedly dressed, and stepped into the closet and opened his small safe to pull out his badge and service weapon. Feeling self consciously like a character in an action movie even as he did it, he checked the magazine and made sure there was a round in the chamber. He'd drawn his gun maybe six times in his career, and never fired a shot outside a range.

Marcie rolled over and pretended to go back to sleep, thinking to herself that her husband was getting sloppy. He'd never let her call him at home in the middle of the night like this. Silent tears of rage and grief fell on her pillow as Gerry staggered out of their room. It was a long time before she managed to actually regain sleep.

Gerry found his briefcase, opened it, and saw that he'd managed to turn off his cell when he tossed it in and dropped a few files on top of it. He turned it on as he shrugged on his overcoat, then nearly dropped it when he heard "Daddy? Is everything ok?"

Veronica stood looking at him, blinking, in her oversize t-shirt. At the oddest moments, despite what he privately recognized as his many failings as a family man, he felt his heart lurch with a kind of desperate love for his strange, wondrous, brilliant daughter. "Yes, honey, everything's fine. What are you doing up?"

"Thirsty, and then I heard you. Where are you going?"

"I need to go take care of something for work that just came up. You go on back to bed, Ronnie." The nickname, despised by her since early adolescence, just slipped out, and actually brought a faint smile to her lips.

"You never call me that anymore."

"You asked me not to. Told me not to, actually. Very, very loudly." He managed a half smile at the memory.

She shuffled forward and hugged him, then said "Go get the bad guys, Dad." and turned to go back to her room.

"I love you, Ronnie." he found himself saying and

meaning.

"Love you, too" huge yawn "Dad. Night. Don't forget we talk about our college trips on Friday." She went back to her room as he cursed to himself and tried to remember what he had scheduled Friday. Some meeting about funding. Well, this time he'd find a way out of it.

After a frantic drive across the city, wholly disregarding speed limits and not using cell phones while driving laws, and hearing a barrage of messages from Craigson, Carter, a sheriff he'd never heard of, and several increasingly high ranking Bureau agents (what had Craigson DONE out there?), he finally arrived at Jill's apartment building. He lost several more minutes trying to find a parking place—flaunting traffic laws at this hour was a worthwhile risk, but it seemed that DC Parking Enforcement never slept, nor would they be likely to cut a sleep-deprived, beset-upon-all-sides FBI agent a break over a no parking zone. He punched in the security code to the lobby doors and raced across to the elevator, fishing in his pocket for his work keys. Hidden between a never used file room key and one that he'd never been quite sure what it was for was the key Jill had long ago given him to her place, with the understanding that he always called first. He was fairly sure he wasn't her only lover, and had never really gotten up the courage to ask.

After what seemed like an endless rise to the seventh floor, Gerry stabbing the button the whole way, the doors finally opened. He tried to force himself to not run and ended up with a shuffling quick-walk that looked utterly ridiculous. At the door, he got the key in the lock on the third try with his somewhat shaking hands and then slowly and carefully drew his weapon. He slammed the door open and yelled "FBI! Don't move!" as he entered, gun at the ready, and then promptly tripped over a lamp chord, bringing the light crashing down and plunging the apartment hallway into darkness. "What the hell?" he said as he managed to not quite fall and not drop his gun.

Outside, a man watching from the street saw the light go out and brought a cell phone to his face. "911? I just heard a guy fighting with his girlfriend, I think he's beating the crap out of her. 4400 Massachusetts Ave, NW, apartment 701. No, I don't wanna give my name, I don't wanna get involved." He hung up the disposable cell, threw it in a nearby trash can, and moved off, pleased with his performance as a panicked neighbor. No doubt Franklin would manage to not be shot by the police, but he should have some very awkward explaining to do, and there was no way he'd be able to keep this a secret now. He slowly walked away, careful to not draw attention to himself, his grey suit blending into the night fairly well.

Elsewhere in the early morning hours, Gina Wright woke up, slipped out of Hector's bed, and found her clothes from the various places they'd been thrown or dropped. She left him a note on the refrigerator door "That was great, call me if you want" with her number, and was careful to not wake him up as she let herself out. She should have plenty of time to get home, feed Cleo the Imperious, Cat of Wonder, get some more sleep, a shower, and get to the station. She wondered if she'd be sent to cover the game that day, and smiled at the thought. She already knew Hector had some good moves, maybe today she'd get to video some of his other ones.

As a shocked Gerry Franklin stood over the bloodied body of Jill Fowler, tied to her bed, clothing ripped away, and carefully reached for his FBI credentials to show the two DC Police Offices who were pointing guns at him, Farris Fakhoury's special alarm clock sounded. The clock actually had a recording of the call to prayer of the faithful from an imam. "Prayer is better than sleep" echoed throughout the room. The clock had been a gift from his mother, Rasheeda. She'd been an ordinary housewife for the majority of Farris' life, until a few years ago. She had first started exploring the

Internet after Farris moved out, and had discovered an incredible, bordering on the uncanny, ability to find things online. At first, she simply amused herself, then began helping her family with things, and now had a sort of unofficial small business, aiding the technologically impaired (or intimidated) in their neighborhood with locating all manner of things on the 'Net, such as the rather odd alarm clock Farris was presently trying to make shut up. As he prepared himself for prayer, he wondered what she'd send next, and hoped she'd stop e-mailing links to various online dating services.

While a somewhat skeptical police sergeant was being told that the suspect in the domestic call was a senior FBI agent, and Farris was finishing his prayers, Mark Holmes woke up. He moved through a short workout routine consisting of push ups, crunches, pull ups, and some Shotokan karate forms he'd recently learned. After showering, he checked his messages and was about to call young Agent Craigson back when the cell rang in his hand. After nearly dropping it, he answered and got an earful from a forensic tech he knew from some seminars about the preliminary exam of Jack Conroy's body, especially about the Arabic character for sword carved into the body twice—the calling card of Nazzir. Finally finished with the call, he debated phoning Ariel, and decided it was a bit early still. He quickly typed up his notes from the call and sent them to her computer, noting that his friend hadn't managed to send along the copies of the report and pictures yet.

A very red-eyed, head-throbbing, hung-over Bucky Buckston glared at his alarm clock as it began playing the local radio morning show he listened to. He'd drunk a bit too much last night, but at least he'd gotten that woman's number. Marge? Marsha? He would find it later, sure it was in his coat pocket. While he tried to slowly get up and not disturb his fragile control over his decidedly unsettled stomach, he suddenly stopped in disbelief. The morning show host was doing his usual host of jokes about yesterday's news, and Buckston was now listening to a bad parody of himself and that god damned "lechislator" slip. Enough was enough. He called in to the station, and left a message with his producer that he'd be out sick today. He rolled over and went back to sleep, having no idea that hangover and ill temper had just saved his life.

The man who called himself Nazzir arrived at his hotel. He was careful in the selection of such places, as he was in every detail of his working life. This was a nice, mid-range place, not a luxury palace nor a hole-in-the-wall, and had a rear entrance that was quite close to a Metro station, greatly expanding his avenues of escape if needed. His second floor room made it unlikely that a petty thief would try and break in the window, and the truly sophisticated masters of such arts would have no reason to come a place like this. Also, a drop from the second floor could be jarring, but easily survivable, and likely without injury barring truly bad luck. And if things truly turned that much against him, well…Insha'Allah as more religiously inclined acquaintances said. The most amusing modern translation of that phrase into English he had heard at a small cafe in Riyadh "God's will—what can you do?" He'd been busy in the last few hours, but he had only one more task for the moment. He used the computer in the lobby, another reason he favored this chain of hotels, and checked a special anonymous e-mail account. His current client had a few more details to relay, and Nazzir responded that he would work them in if he could, but that last minute additions were never a good tactical decision. He also added his thanks for the caution about Conroy's pistol skill. Retired and taken by surprise, the former agent had still managed to produce a pistol from under his jacket and even get a shot off before Nazzir dropped him. The man must have been extraordinary. It was a sad thing to remove such talent from the world, but it was a very good idea to not let that particular talent into a position of advantage. Nazzir was very good at what he did, but he had no doubt that in a "fair" fight, whatever that was, Conroy would have bested him with pistols at the very least. After torturing some more recent information from Conroy and then paying a call on Jill Fowler, Nazzir had stuck around long enough only to call the local police, and then slowly walked away. Now, he left a wake up call at the desk and returned to his room. He had a great deal to do today, but some time yet before he was needed, and as he read in a spy thriller once, "rest is a weapon." He lay down and closed his eyes and slid instantly into untroubled sleep, a skill soldiers the world over develop quickly.

Elsewhere, various men with roles to play that day finished their morning prayers in different locations. Very few of them had ever met, and none associated with the other. Many were wholly ignorant of anything about the others. One man began a series of special breathing exercises he had learned with his particular training, and reached a hand out to almost lovingly caress the long case, carefully decorated with artistically applied paint smears. He would find his nest later that day, and bring down the Wrath of Allah from above. A special group of volunteers who could not serve in a more direct way in the fight went over their specially prepared fliers and boxes filled with the great weakness of law enforcement everywhere. Even the humblest of positions may serve in unexpected ways, and a man went to work as normal, with a special stop planned before he radically altered his delivery route. Others enjoyed a specially prepared lavish breakfast as they made ready their thoughts for special videos to be filmed before they set out to catch their train.

The man who had once had a brother named Fadi Hadad completed his prayers and returned to his small rented room. He had spent years putting the pieces of this together, and today was the day—his vengeance was at hand. He had recruited in several different ways—by ideology, politics, desire for revenge, and in some cases, simply by payment, but things had finally begun. The first few deaths were mostly incidental, stage dressing, if you will. The later events of today would speak loudly, and the clamor they would raise would swallow the small disturbances of these opening salvos. He dozed a bit in his chair, his sleep tormented by images of his lost brother, hints of things forgotten, and anticipation of what was to come.

Jennie Doorfner left her home to go to her usual early morning church service. Her devotions sometimes caused her to be a bit late for work, but she had long ago explained her situation to Agent Franklin, and he had agreed that a few lost minutes on some mornings could be easily made up by her rarely taking lunch breaks, and indeed rarely taking vacation time. She sometimes went on a retreat with her church, but those were almost always weekend affairs. Once a year, she and a few close friends made what they called their Pilgrimage, and drove from the Washington area down to Graceland. Jesus was Lord with Jennie Doorfner, there was no question of that, but Elvis was a respectable second. Lou Doorfner's place in her hierarchy had been settled several years ago, when Jesus had seen fit to call him home while he was repairing a sink in one of the city Youth Centers. He had earned a good living as a plumber, and both the city and the union and been very generous when he died on the job. That, coupled with Jennie's modest lifestyle, left her comfortably well off in her late middle age. She made her way into the church, reminding herself to say a special prayer for poor Agent Franklin. He was such an understanding supervisor, and he'd had no end of trouble with that rascal of a brother of his, and it sounded like he'd really made a mess of things this time…but she shouldn't judge, of course. That was His place, not hers. She found her place in a pew and tried to clear her thoughts of murdering drug-addict brothers and flighty interns who went running off with good looking young agents with no explanation…not that she needed one.

Ariel Hanson had worked hard on her information projects. She had computer programs she was fine-tuning to search for certain words and phrases, and automated alerts about certain kinds of reports from every agency she could get access to. She had worked assiduously to establish a network of contacts to keep her up to date or give her a heads up on various types of events. Which is why she was surprised, in the few moments she had later to look back, that her first real indication of the events of the day came from the local news. After her alarm had summoned her from a very comfortable sleep, she had moved out to the kitchen, taken a cup of coffee from the coffee maker, which she had remembered to actually fill *AND* set the timer on for once. Sitting down with her first mug of the day, she turned on the poorly-named "24 Hour Local News" channel, breathing a sigh of relief when she saw the various overnight infomercials were done. What immediately captured her attention was a live broadcast outside an apartment building in the Northwest part of the city, where there was a ".breaking news about a woman murdered in her apartment. The woman's identity has not been released to the public pending notification of her relatives, but neighbors have said she worked for the FBI. Further, an anonymous police source has said that a man is being questioned in regards to her death, and that he, too, works for the FBI." This was enough to send Ariel diving for both her cell and her computer. She brought up her email, and noticed a message from Holmes with a number of attachments. Ariel quickly brought herself up to speed on the death of Jack Conroy, but noticed that his address was a rural one, and that he was definitely male, so he couldn't be the dead woman in Northwest DC. Finally, exasperated, she reached out to a friend on the DC Police force who she had met at a computer show for government agencies. Agreeing to not reveal his name to anyone, ever, she finally got Jill Fowler's relevant information, but he either didn't know or wouldn't say who was being questioned. Well, it seemed like if she was going to find out what was going on, she'd need to be a bit more official than an oversize t-shirt and scuffed up slippers. She gulped down the rest of her coffee and rushed off for the shower, hoping her thermos was clean for the rest of that coffee.

The Day Of

Mid- To Late-Morning

Wanda came into Bernie's office, carrying two coffees. "I didn't have enough hands for bagels. Did I do something? You don't usually call me in to your office, you usually tell me to go away." She took a steadying breath, realizing she was babbling, and held out the coffee in her right hand. "Black, one sugar."

"Thanks." He sipped once and motioned for her to sit. "No, you didn't do anything. But you will."

She looked back at him, confused, as she took her own swig of coffee. "I…what?"

"He says he's sick—I'm betting equal parts hangover and jokes about this whole 'lechislator' bit—but Bucky's not coming in today. So…we need someone to cover the Senator's Day Game. Not exactly an anchor job, but better than traffic spots, right?"

She nearly choked. "What? You're giving me the game?"

He looked across the desk at her. "Well, if you want it. You interested?"

She would hotly deny it later, and take offense to the term, but Wanda squealed. "Omigod of COURSE I'm interested! Thank you!" He slid the file of what had been prepared already to her, and she grabbed it up, quickly running back to her own desk, while Bernie smiled.

"Kinda thought you might be," he said, shaking his head once and going back over his paperwork.

Lisa Carter got to the office, feeling the worse for wear from her late night, and wondering if anything new had happened. While she'd done her best to play herself off as not rattled by her and Agent Craigson's discovery last night, it had shaken her a bit and she'd slept poorly in the not quite enough time she had for it. She moved over to the small table she'd been using as an improvised desk for her internship, and felt Mrs. Doorfner glaring at her. "Your internship starts at nine, young lady," the older woman's voice grated a bit on Lisa's ears.

Lisa fought the urge to snap at her and stifled a yawn. "Agent Craigson and I got back very late last night, Mrs. Doorfner." she began, only to be interrupted.

"Your social life is not my concern, or interest. Your basic duties are spelled out in your Intern Agreement, and if you can't stick to that, we can get another intern easily. You were very lucky to get this placement."

Lisa gritted her teeth against the barrage of self righteousness and faulty conclusions. She slowly counted down from five in her head and then held up her hand in a stop gesture. "Mrs. Doorfner, I think you have the wrong idea."

"Don't you start telling me about your family connections, young lady, I know who you're related to. Everyone does. It doesn't change anything as far as I'm concerned."

Lisa took another deep breath. "All right, Mrs. Doorfner, just hold up a moment. First off, I didn't ask my grandfather to help me get this. I can't help who I'm related to. Second," she held up another finger, seeing Mrs. Doorfner's face register displeasure and pushing on anyway "I've been very professional and taken this seriously since I started here, and you've never missed an opportunity to criticize me anyway, and third," she saw the change on Jennie's face to anger and pushed on, "if you're implying what it sounds like you are, I wasn't on a date with Agent Craigson. Agent Franklin sent us out to check on his friend Jack Conroy, and I was hoping to find out why."

Mrs. Doorfner's face now showed confusion. "He sent you out? He wouldn't do that, you're an intern." Her voice sounded much weaker and less shrill than a moment ago.

"Yes, that was mentioned several times." Her face took on a wry look. "Is Agent Franklin in? I have some messages for him."

"No, he said he would be late today" Mrs. Doorfner sounded at least less hostile. "I suppose it has something to do with his brother, poor man."

"Did something happen with his brother?" Lisa was both a bit concerned and somewhat confused. What else had happened to Franklin yesterday, and was this why he was so wound up in the late afternoon?

"His brother is a...troubled soul, I suppose I can tell you in confidence. Agent Franklin has hoped he would pull himself together for years now, and there was a setback, you could call it, yesterday." She looked hurriedly around. "You need to keep this to yourself, of course."

Lisa agreed, distracted. She wondered what had happened with the brother, and was glad Mrs. Doorfner hadn't asked about Conroy. She didn't want to have to tell her, and no doubt hear some string of Bible quotes about death and such things. As a peace offering, and to get out of the conversation, Lisa said "I was going to get more coffee. Would you like some?" After getting the specifications on how she liked it (just like $EVERY$ time, Lisa thought), she moved down the hall to the coffee room/kitchen.

Mark Holmes sat at his desk, having come in early after the late night (or early morning) call about the murder. He'd finally gotten some of the pictures of Agent Conroy's body, and it certainly looked like the work of Nazzir. He looked up at the knock on his door. "Yes?"

Martha Chen stuck her head in the door. She'd worked with Holmes a few times, and knew both that he had a first rate mind and that he isolated himself from the office gossip pool enough that he probably didn't know. "Did you hear about Jill Fowler?"

He looked at her for a moment. "Cute brunette in Forensics…computers or something? What about her?"

"Accounting, not computers. And she got killed last night."

"Last night? When? What happened?" Holmes straightened up, focusing a lot more intently on her.

"She was found dead in her apartment. And they're saying that one of us found her, but no one's saying who. Thought you might want to know. We're getting flowers for the funeral, whenever they do that."

Holmes was up and moving already. He grabbed his wallet out of his pocket and hurriedly tossed her a bill without looking at it. "Thanks, I need to check on something." He walked past her and on down the hall, pulling his cell off his belt as he went.

Agent Chen shook her head. Holmes was a brilliant guy, but rather lacking in social graces. At least he'd kicked in for the flowers before he ran off. She glanced at the money in her hand. He probably hadn't meant to give her a fifty, though. Martha picked up a sticky pad, left him a quick note and stuck it to the computer monitor, then went off to continue her rounds about the collection for poor Jill.

Craigson was just walking off the elevator when his cell chimed. He glanced at the number, not recognizing it, and answered. "Craigson." as he moved down the corridor towards his office. He tried to fight off the huge yawn he felt coming. After some resistance rooted in southern manners, he'd finally persuaded Lisa to get some sleep on the drive back, but he was really feeling the late night and grisly discovery.

"Agent Craigson, this is Mark Holmes. I got your message and I need to ask you some follow up questions. Are you in the office?"

"Yeah. I mean, yes sir. I'm in 504, but I can meet you somewhere else if that's better."

"No, just stay there. I'm on my way." Holmes hung up and then for the second time that day felt the phone pulse in his hand, once more almost dropping it. For some reason, the feeling of the buzzing setting always unnerved him. Muttering "Don't *DO* that," at the cell, he flipped it open. "Holmes."

"Mark, it's Ariel. I've got some stuff I need to talk with you about." she began.

"If it's about last night, I'm looking at few things myself. You want to come over to Counter-Terrorism?" he suggested.

"Sure, I'm on my way." They hung up and Holmes continued on his way.

Craigson heard the click of disconnection and shrugged. At least he could get some coffee first. Pouring himself some, he decided to grab another mug and carried them both back to his small cubicle. Just as he sat down, he heard rapid footsteps moving towards him. He gulped down a mouthful of coffee hurriedly and then saw the somewhat older man peering in at him. "Agent Craigson?"

"Yes sir. Good to see you again, Agent Holmes." The two shook hands. "How can I help you sir? I don't think I have anything more to add than the interviews last night. I was just the one who found the body. That was a bad one, helluva way to go out, especially for someone who was one of us."

"I just ran across some more information, actually. Do you know if there's any connection between Conroy and Agent Jill Fowler? She works with the Forensic Accounting section." Holmes saw a flicker of recognition in Craigson' eyes. "Conroy? No, I don't think so. Well, not directly anyway."

"There's an indirect one? What is it, Agent Craigson?" Holmes noted the young man looking very uncomfortable and wondered what was making him feel that way about a fairly simple question.

"Well.umm...Look...I'm going to tell you anyway, but can you leave out where you heard this from? I'd rather not get a rep for talking about my fellow agents." Holmes waved his hand in a dismissive motion, then made a 'go on' gesture. "Ok, well, Conroy was some kind of teacher or something to Agent Franklin....you know who I mean?"

Holmes looked over at him. "Paperclip?"

Craigson laughed then smothered the smile. "Yeah, him. Anyway, so he and Conroy were friends too, or something, did a lot of stuff together. Fowler." he looked around, standing up and peering over his cubicle walls like a prairie dog before sitting down again. "Franklin and Fowler had a thing going on, I'm about positive."

Holmes looked surprised. "They had an affair?"

Craigson nodded. "Yeah, for a long time, or I'm pretty sure anyway. I'm sort of assigned to work with Franklin, so I'm over in his office a lot. That's why I got sent out to Conroy's place, I guess—well, me and Lisa."

"Who's Lisa?" Holmes hadn't read all the file, being more concerned with the pictures and the Nazzir angle.

"Lisa Carter, she's an intern-" he saw the look Holmes was giving him "I know, I know, it wasn't my idea, Franklin told me to take her. He was kinda not making a lot of sense, and wasn't really listening, you know?"

"And Lisa is interning for Franklin? Who was having an affair with Fowler?" Craigson nodded twice. "Ok, come on. We're going to go talk to Paperclip."

Craigson managed to not laugh this time as he got up. "Ok, but you gotta stop calling him that. At least in front of me. He *HATES* that name."

Holmes flashed the young agent a quick smile. "I know."

Holmes and Craigson walked into Franklin's office at the same time that Lisa returned with the coffees for her and Jennie. "Hi, Ron" she said in greeting as she placed one of the mugs on Mrs. Doorfner's desk. "There you go," she said, turning back to the new comers. As she opened her mouth to speak, she was a bit surprised to hear Mrs. Doorfner behind her.

"Agent Holmes. What brings you here?" The voice was rarely pleasant to most people, but now would have dripped with scorn if it hadn't been frozen solid by the glacial chill in her tone.

He smiled down at her. "Still here, Jennie? I need to talk to Agent Franklin about an investigation."

"It's Mrs. Doorfner, and you should have called and made an appointment," she replied.

"Well, it just came up. So, is he here?" Holmes stood looking at her, apparently not much more fond of her than she of him.

"If you had bothered to call ahead, you would have saved yourself a trip, and found out that he's going to be in late this morning." They glared at each other for a moment, the tension broken when Ariel found them. "Oh, here you are, I thought you were in your office," her voice trailed off as she took in the scene. "Everything ok?"

"Sure, it's great." Holmes turned to her and took her aside as the intern and rookie agent exchanged glances.

In a rapid whisper and low tones, Holmes brought Ariel up to speed on what he'd found so far, then looked back over his shoulder. "Try and get the intern off somewhere, would you? Ask her about Franklin and Fowler. I'll deal with the Dragon Lady."

"Why me?" Ariel asked, looking at the young woman who was put together in the kind of casual elegance that Ariel knew she could never come close to.

"Do some of that girl talk stuff." He winked at her look. "I know you can do it."

Grumbling, Ariel thought a moment and took a gamble. She walked over to the admin's desk "Excuse me, Mrs. Doorfner" she said, reading the name off the desk plate "Could you tell me where the ladies' room is?"

"Lisa, why don't you show her the way?" Jennie directed.

Lisa put down her coffee with a concealed sigh and said "Sure, come on, it's this way." leading the DHS agent down the hall.

As they left, they heard Holmes saying "So where's Gerry? He's almost always here."

Lisa shook her head as they went into the restroom. "I know she doesn't get on with a lot of people, but that's about the worst I've seen her."

Ariel laughed. "Mark can rub a lot of people the wrong way, and sometimes he does it on purpose."

"So, since I'm betting you can read, what did you want to ask me away from Mrs. D?" Lisa asked, regarding the other woman.

"You're quick. That's good. We heard something about Franklin and Agent Jill Fowler seeing each other. Do you know anything about that?" Ariel asked.

"Oh, yeah, that would be a bad question in front of her. Fowler, huh?" Lisa appeared to give the question some thought for a few moments. "I could see it. I hadn't heard anything about it, but I do see her over here sometimes. What brought that up? I doubt you're over here checking up on the rumor mill."

Ariel heard the humor in her voice and said, "I take it you haven't heard?"

"Heard what? About those two? I just told you no." Lisa studied her face a moment. "But that's not what you meant. What happened?"

As Ariel told Lisa about the murder last night, Craigson

was trying to find an excuse to leave, although a part of him was fascinated by the exchange between Holmes and Doorfner. They were both being polite enough on paper—if you'd seen a transcript of their conversation, you wouldn't think anything of it. But hearing the tones, watching the body language, there was something here that was ugly, lurking under a very thin veneer of civil conversation.

"So you don't know where he is, why he's late, or why he's not answering his cell phone?" Holmes was a step or two back from the desk but somehow gave the impression of looming over her.

"Agent Franklin is a very busy man, and he doesn't need to clear his schedule with me," she answered, just short of snapping back at him.

"Clear it, no. But I believe it's customary to at least check in from time to time, let your office know if you're going to be out, and if so, why." Holmes' tone was flat, and he was clearly not overly impressed with the woman's evasions.

"I really don't have to explain myself, or Agent Franklin, to you, Agent Holmes." Mrs. Doorfner, not being able to intimidate the man with her usual array of angry looks or references to Franklin's importance, was falling back on stonewalling.

"No, you don't. I'll be in touch." Holmes turned and stopped as Ariel and Lisa came back in.

"Agent Hanson, if you'd accompany me, we seem to be done here for now. Agent Craigson, you're with us." Holmes directed as he moved toward the door.

"Agent Craigson is assigned to work with this office," Mrs. Doorfner said haughtily.

"If he happens to call in and complain about it, have Agent Franklin call me." Holmes dropped one of his cards on her desk. "In the meanwhile, admin assistants can't assign agents, so you can't use him, and I can. Good morning, Mrs. Doorfner." He calmly walked out, the other two agents trailing after him. Lisa had the good sense to industriously appear to be filing when Doorfner looked around, and the older woman sniffed at her desk, muttering things Lisa thought she was just as glad she couldn't hear.

Jon Lasalle woke up and squinted at his clock. Plenty of time. This was supposed to be his day off, but he was senior enough that when the call went out about overtime available at the special Washington Nationals game today, he'd been able to snag a spot for himself. He sat up and stretched, stumbling off for the shower, making sure he had a clean uniform ready to go on the way. He wondered who else had signed up, and shook his head. He'd find out later, and any day a single cop can make extra OT was a good one. Cheered by the prospect of the anticipated easy money, he whistled off key and badly as he showered. No one complained—no one had been there to for the last several years after he and his wife split. He got some breakfast and turned on the news, checking to see if there was anything that looked likely to screw up his day. The murder in Northwest sounded like an ugly one, but he didn't work that part of the city and wasn't homicide. He vaguely wondered who this "unnamed suspect" was they seemed to have caught on scene, and toyed with the idea of finding out as he ate his cereal.

The man called Nazzir awoke and checked his clock. As usual, it was approximately five minutes before he wanted to get up. He had developed this trick some years ago, and found it very useful. He rose and went through some light exercise, stopping to play the sleep befuddled business man who'd been out too late when his wake up call came. After a shower, he reviewed his plans for the day. So much to do, and so little time. Fortunately, he'd always been a skilled organizer. He packed his simple bag and stood still a moment, pondering setting the room on fire. It wasn't a part of the assignment, but might kick the festivities off early. He decided not to—he hadn't been given instructions to, and didn't need to draw attention to himself. Besides, the hotel restaurant was actually good and reasonably priced, not always easy to come by in this day and age. He left and went through the ritual of signing out at the desk, walking off to the nearby Metro station.

Hector Valdez woke up and smiled, images from last night replaying themselves in his mind. He was also happy to see she had left as he'd asked. It had nothing to do with her, or the sex, which had been great. On game days, he liked to wake up alone and focus himself. He was allowed to skip some practices and warm ups as long as he continued to turn in the stellar performances he had been. He moved to the kitchen to get some bottled water and saw her note, and smiled more. He likely would call her again, she'd been a lot of fun and didn't seem to take things too seriously. Sipping his water, before he began the discipline of getting himself into his zone, he let his mind wander a bit. He'd known he had a gift since he was seven years old, the first time he'd really played a game of baseball. Some kids in the neighborhood were short a player, and decided to let him fill in. To everyone's surprise, including his own, he went from mascot to MVP of the game, pulling off plays that left boys a good five years or more older stunned. He'd been blessed with a special talent, and then he decided that wasn't enough, and he worked at it. Every day, he'd thrown whatever balls he could scrounge at make-shift targets. He'd practiced. He'd watched games not just because he loved them, which he did, but because he was studying the players. He began to surprise his father's friends when they came over to watch, analyzing the plays with seriousness and insight far beyond his years. He played in high school of course, and Little League before that. No one was surprised when he was scouted by an agent, and he slowly worked his way up to the big leagues. His mother asked him once if he shouldn't go to college, and he said "Mama, this is what I want to do, all I want to do, I think it is why God put me here. Why make Him wait?" She had laughed at her precocious son and agreed to not oppose his career choice.

When he finally did make the majors, he avoided many of the traps other young players fell into. He helped his parents with their bills, because it was the duty of a son, and they had been good parents. He had no interest in buying flashy cars, and a few beers was all he ever really felt the need to drink. He had gifts, and knew it, but had weaknesses as well, and knew that. His big brother would never be a professional ball player, but he could make sense of the sheets of numbers that told Hector what he was making, and how, and where it went. His brother managed the money carefully, and paid himself a very modest fee for it (you don't steal from family, and he was only paid at all because Hector insisted). There were things that Hector felt about his playing he had trouble articulating. It wasn't just that his English wasn't the best, it was more he had never really been an introspective man, and wasn't sure how to describe what he felt.

Baseball was all he had ever felt he was good at it, the only thing he really felt he excelled at. He was grateful every day that he was allowed to make a living doing something he loved. He made a very good living, and he knew that too. The money was great, but not why he played, and the celebrity was at times unnerving. His wealth allowed him to care for his family, and occasionally do something for one his friends from the neighborhood. The kid who'd first asked him to play had tickets to any game he played in, and if the management wouldn't spring for complimentary ones, he'd buy them himself. He had a few times, too, until a reporter for Sport Illustrated had gotten hold of the story, and written a scathing article making the owners look like incredible cheapskates. Hector has been accused of leaking the story, but as he himself said in an interview with one of the late night hosts "I'm not that smart, I just throw baseballs." But he'd laughed when he read the article, and had sent the reporter a case of his favorite whiskey at Christmas. What really kept him playing, and made him try so hard, and agree to so many special events and appearances, were the fans. Not the ones that were almost stalkers, or the ones that roared his name at the games. But the ones that just loved the game, and were loyal to their team, and appreciated his skill. He felt protective of them, they were *HIS* fans, not that they belonged to him, but that he owed them, and so he played his heart out, and tried to get his teammates to as well. He had no delusions that the team was doing well just because of him. He played with some great men, and he knew it, and at times found ways to express it to them. Some didn't understand, and some made fun of him, but when one would look at him a little differently, and then nod slowly and smile, he felt it was worth all the ridicule of the ones that just didn't get it. Of course, he'd have to admit, some of the benefits were fantastic, as his wandering mind returned to last night's escapades and he finally pulled himself up to start getting into the zone.

Jennie Doorfner would never admit it, certainly not in front a young intern like Lisa Carter, but she wasn't really sure what to do. Several people had called asking about Agent Franklin, and she didn't really know what to tell them. The message he had left on her voice mail was short and not really informative, and he hadn't answered any of her calls since then. She was getting worried about him. Between what she'd learned yesterday about his brother, and then the death of Conroy, who had in ways been like a father to him, she was concerned that he might be feeling overwhelmed. She looked up suddenly at an unexpected footfall, wondering if that irritating Holmes had returned, and then saw who it was. "Oh, Agent Franklin, I'm glad you're here. You've had a lot of people looking for you," her voice trailed off when she got a better look at him. He looked horrible. He needed a shave, his suit was wrinkled, and his eyes bloodshot.

He looked at her blankly for a moment and then said "No calls right now," and went into his office and slowly closed the door. Jennie stared after him, again at a loss. Lisa, who had seen the exchange, was up and moving already.

"I need to take these down to the file room, do you need anything?" She waved a stack of papers at Mrs. Doorfner, who shook her head. Lisa walked quickly down to the file room and moved to the very back, then pulled out her cell and found the card she'd made sure to get last night. After punching in the number, she waited for the pick up and then said "Hey, Ron? Are you still with Agent Holmes? Ok, tell him I thought he might want to know that Franklin just came in, and he looks like hell. See you later." She hung up and did her actual filing, then returned to her desk.

In his office, Franklin sat dazed, staring at nothing. He was beyond terrified—he was numb by now. A creeping sense of dread was gnawing at him, had been since he'd gotten that call reminding him about the Hadad arrest. He'd made his career off that, and had even convinced himself he'd done everything right. The small gaps, the doubts, he'd pushed them all aside and had told the story so often he'd even come to believe it himself. And then that phone call. And now all this. He still couldn't believe Jill was dead, that he'd seen her like that, all the blood. Then the police, and their questions, and their suspicions. It had been one of, if not the, worst nights of his life. It had taken hours to convince them to let him go, and he was sure the lead detective, Harrison, was nowhere near done with him. There were reports he should write, notifications he should make, calls to place, and messages to check, but somehow it all seemed more effort that it was worth. So he just sat there, waiting for something else to happen, to be pushed in another direction. He stared at the phone, half hoping it would ring, and half praying it wouldn't. Jill had been a wonderful, smart, energetic, driven woman, and he'd never understood why she was interested in him. And now she was gone, just because someone wanted to prove some kind of point, or torture him in some way? Well, it was working. He felt totally beaten. A small part of him wondered how long it would be before he was placed on suspension "pending further investigation." He tried to look ahead, and saw his career in ruins, his reputation shattered, and everything he'd worked for gone. He wondered 'what next?' and then shuddered at the thought and lay his head down on his desk.

Farris Fakhoury drove his cruiser along the city streets. He still wasn't quite used to it, and every once in a while caught himself grinning like an idiot. He'd been hired, made it through the Academy, passed all the tests along the way, and Rafe had finally passed him through his Field Training. Officer Fakhoury, it had a ring to it, at least as far as he was concerned. His reverie was interrupted by the squawking of his radio. "435?"

He keyed his mic. "435, go."

"435, call in at your convenience."

He wondered what that was about, and pulled over when he saw a clear space. Pulling out his cell phone, he called the dispatcher, who put him on hold. He was a bit surprised when he found himself talking to Sgt. Ranier. "Fakhoury, how're doing?" The sergeant asked.

Somewhat impressed that the man had managed to pronounce his name right, he said "Fine, sir. It's good."

The sergeant chuckled a little. "I remember my first few months after getting cut loose. Nothing like it. Having fun out there?"

He wondered where this was going, but said "Yes, sir, I am. Like you said, there's nothing like it."

"Wanna have some more fun?" The question threw him a bit.

"Sir?" Fakhoury asked, a bit confused.

"We're short on mid-day. Can you stay for some O.T.?" The sergeant asked him.

Fakhoury thought about it. He'd been looking forward to getting off shift and going home, but the extra money was always good, and it might not be a bad idea to get on his supervisor's good side. "Yeah, sure, Sarge. I can stay."

"Great. We'll just keep you out in that car for now, and see what we need to shuffle around later. Thanks, Fakhoury. Watch your computer, we can send you anything that pops up in roll call if you need it."

Fakhoury ended the phone call and decided if he was staying on that long, he needed a real lunch today, not his usual small break. So he radioed in to be put on the break list and went back to work, waiting his turn.

Wanda had been hoping for a big break, and this seemed like it was at least a step in the right direction. She'd spent some time doing some ecstatic, but frantic, planning, and then looked up when she noticed someone standing by her desk.

"Hi, Gina Wright. I'm going to be running camera for you."

"Wanda Fullbright, I think I've seen you around. Hope you don't mind not working with Bucky today."

Gina regarded her a moment. "You gonna breathe booze fumes all over me?"

Wanda held her hand up in front of her mouth and made a big show of exhaling and sniffing. "No, doesn't seem like it."

"You gonna hit on me while we're trying to work?" Gina was still looking at her with a hard to read expression.

"Sorry, I'm straight." Wanda answered.

Gina smiled. "Then no, I don't mind." They shook hands, and Wanda indicated the spare chair, for once not covered in files and papers.

"Now let me tell you what I was thinking about and see

what you think." They moved their heads together and began plotting.

Gerry was vaguely aware of raised voices just outside his office door. He could hear Jennie, and then another voice that was sort of familiar, but wasn't worth the effort of placing it. A few other voices from time to time were trying to calm the first two, he thought distractedly. Finally, there was a much louder shout from Jennie and Gerry's door was flung open. He looked at a tall, thin, nicely dressed black man, and his not quite clear mind spat out a name. "Agent Holmes." It was more statement than greeting. With Holmes was the seemingly omnipresent young Agent Craigson, and a woman he didn't think he knew. He looked at them dully.

"I had a few things I needed to ask you about, now that you're here, Franklin" Holmes said, a tone of combativeness in his voice.

"All right." Franklin's voice was flat and toneless, the customary edge of near condescension missing. Holmes looked a bit surprised, and shot a look at the woman. They all stepped in and closed the door on Jennie's ineffectual protests.

"You seem like you have a lot happening all around you all of a sudden, Franklin. So what's going on?" Holmes remained standing, arms folded across his chest.

"Jill's dead." he said in that same flat voice.

"Yes, Jill's dead. And from some pictures I saw, it looks like she was killed by a guy called Nazzir, who tends to only do high end terrorism. So why is he here and killing people around you?" Holmes pressed.

"People? What do you mean?" There was a flicker of awareness, intelligence, behind Gerry's mostly dead eyes.

Holmes looked at Craigson, who held up his hands in a warding gesture and said "I left him six messages, and from the tone of the people asking me questions last night, I wasn't the only one. I thought he knew. He should know."

Holmes mentally shifted gears, eyeing the seated man and starting to wonder how much he was actually taking in. "Gerry, I'm sorry, I'm not real good at this kind of thing. Jack Conroy is dead." The woman winced at the bald statement.

"Jack?" Gerry looked up for the first time, meeting Holmes' gaze. "What happened?"

"He was killed, Gerry. It looks like by the same man who killed Jill. He uses a small blade to mark his victims with an Arabic character, like a signature, when he has time. That mark was found on both bodies. I'm sorry. Do you know why someone would send him after you? I don't think he's a real true believer, I think he usually works for money, and doesn't come cheap." Holmes paused, waiting.

"They called me." It was murmured, hard to hear.

"What? What did you say, Jerry?" Holmes' voice was sharp now, curious.

"They called me. Once, years ago, the day we caught Hadad. Then again, yesterday. Right after that sheriff called me about Harry, they called me on Jack's phone."

The three exchanged looks and Holmes leaned a bit forward, hands resting on Gerry's desk now.

"Who called you, and what did they say? Each time, Gerry, this is important."

The man behind the desk seemed like he was making an effort to gather his thoughts. "I got a call on Jill's phone, telling me to come look for myself. So I went over, and found her body, and then the police burst in behind me, and I've been dealing with them all morning."

Holmes and Hanson exchanged a look at the revelation that Gerry had been the one to find the body.

"What did the voice sound like, Gerry?" Holmes asked.

"Computer disguised, like the other call." came the response.

"What other call?"

"Yesterday afternoon," he paused and rubbed his face,

"was it really only yesterday? Seems so much longer ago…I got that call from the sheriff about my brother, then my cell rang, and it was Jack's number. But it wasn't Jack. It was that computer voice, saying that their promise was being kept, or something like that. So, I sent Craigson and Carter out to check on Jack, because they're both so damn cheerful and upbeat and eager and I needed them somewhere else for a while so I could think. Jack's really dead?" He looked up and met Holmes' gaze for the second time. Unnoticed, Craigson slipped out of the room.

"Yes, he is. So, the person calling you used a computer scrambler for their voice. Did he say anything else?" Holmes eyed Gerry, trying to get a read on the man's emotional state.

"No, not really."

"Were those the only two calls?" Holmes saw something shift in the man's face and knew he was on the right track.

"No." his voice trailed off and he sat silently for a few moments.

Silence could be useful as an interrogation technique, but this wasn't that sort of talk, and Holmes had a feeling time was important. "What were the other calls, Gerry?" he prompted.

"One. There was just one. The day we got Hadad." Holmes nodded, recalling the arrest, the one that was supposed to disrupt terrorist funding, but hadn't, and that made Gerry's career here. He made a gesture for him to continue. "I got called that evening, late afternoon I guess. No computer stuff on this one. He had a deep voice, sounded sort of British or something…he talked to me about the arrest, and said I had the wrong man. We argued a bit, and he finally said that he was the one I was looking for, that I had his brother, and that he'd make a deal with me to turn himself in if I let his brother go." Gerry seemed to wind down, as if his small stock of energy had run out relating this.

"So what did you say, Gerry?" Holmes asked, a bit

quieter, fairly certain he knew roughly what the answer would be.

"I said we didn't negotiate with terrorists, that I had the right person, that the evidence all pointed to him, and that if he wanted to talk about surrendering, I'd set up a time and place for him." Holmes closed his eyes, wondering how much that answer and attitude would cost, then thought of Conroy and Fowler and realized the price was already too high. "The evidence did point to the Hadads, and everything I could find made it seem like it was Fadi Hadad who was the big financier. And when we took him, he was a textbook case, saying things like death to America, and that if we killed him, he'd just be a martyr, and that we couldn't stop the righteous, all manner of things like that. It all fit, it all pointed to him, and he never denied it!" Gerry's voice had taken on an almost pleading tone. "It all made sense, don't you see?"

"Yes, Gerry. I see." Holmes rubbed the bridge of his nose and then looked around, seemingly at a loss. "Did they give you any idea what they were going to do, what they had planned?" His eyes roamed the walls, the pictures of Gerry at various awards dinners, meeting politicians, at a fund raiser and the grand re-opening of the Smithsonian American History Museum.

"No. He just said he'd make me pay, or make me regret it, and that Fadi was the only family he had, or something like that." Gerry shook his head and slumped in his chair.

"Gerry, I can't tell you what to do here, but I'm going to make some suggestions, OK? I think you should just stay here, call me if you think of anything else," Holmes placed a card on Franklin's desk, "and sit tight a while." Gerry nodded a bit jerkily.

Holmes motioned to Ariel, and they left, closing the door behind them. Holmes crossed to Jennie's desk and then stunned her. "I'm in a hurry, so I'll be blunt. We don't like each other, fine. I don't like him much, either," he jerked his thumb at Franklin's closed office door. "But I think he's had a series of shocks over the last day or so, and he's not doing too well with them. You might want to keep an eye on him." Mrs. Doorfner's mouth opened, but nothing came out as she stared at Holmes. "Ok, people, we have work to do. Hanson, Craigson, come with me." They left behind them a flabbergasted Mrs. Doorfner, and Lisa Carter, who was wondering if this was a very bad or very good time to be an intern here.

The three agents moved down the hall towards the conference rooms, Holmes opening doors at random until he found one not being used. He brought them in and sat everyone down, leaning back in one of the chairs and letting his breath out in a loud whoosh. "Anyone else think that sounded bad?"

Ariel nodded. "I don't think whoever they are set all this up just to kill off two people connected to Franklin. I think there's more coming."

Holmes agreed. "We need to find out what that deal with the sheriff was that he kept mentioning."

Craigson smiled and pulled out a note pad. "Lisa heard most of this yesterday. Franklin's brother is Harry, supposed to have a record for all kinds of small time drug offenses. Yesterday, this sheriff calls and says that Harry's been arrested for more drug charges, but murder this time, too. The theory is that he got into a fight with his dealer."

Holmes nodded approvingly. "Good job. Do you have the sheriff's contact information?" Craigson tore off a page and slid it over to the senior agent. "Great. Ok, we need to find out what happened with his brother, I doubt this is a coincidence, it's too much at once." Holmes laid out a series of avenues to explore. He had a skilled mind for investigation, and many resources. Ariel, too, was an adept researcher and investigator, and had access to some areas Holmes did not. Craigson had a great deal of potential, and an open enough mind to learn from two such talented people. Unfortunately for all of them, they were already too late.

The Day Of

It Begins

Peter Dylan was the desk sergeant for the 5th District station. He handled various complaints and public relations, and tried to remember sometimes that he was really still a cop. It didn't feel like it with the kind of bullshit they had him dealing with a lot of the time. A man in a suit walked in and approached his desk—but unlike many of the people who came in, he was smiling. "Excuse me, Sergeant, I believe I am supposed to speak with you?" His accent was foreign, but not one Dylan immediately recognized. He put on a polite expression and wondered what was up this time.

"How can I help you, sir?" He asked.

"I am part of the Neighborhood Involvement Committee for my area," the man began

'Oh, God, now what? More Neighborhood Watch type guys to tell us how to do our job, or beg equipment? Complaints about the local cops?' Dylan thought, nodding and smiling.

"We have been discussing the fine job our assigned officers have been doing for us lately, and we wished to show our appreciation." Dylan looked at him, hiding his surprise. Maybe this wouldn't be so bad. "I believe, at least I hope it is not simply a hateful stereotype, but I believe certain things are favored by your officers?"

Dylan was now verging on confused—was this man going to try and bribe them? "Like what, sir?" he asked, keeping his voice neutral.

"We have purchased several boxes of donuts—they are in my car. If this is acceptable, we wished to give them to you, as something to start your shift off with. A token of our esteem? Is this all right?" The man looked at the Sergeant questioningly.

"Well....it's a little irregular, but I guess it would be all right this time. And thank you very much, Mister.?"

The man smiled and extended his hand. "Ammar Hadad." Arrangements were quickly made to have an officer or two help bring them in, and get them distributed to the roll call room for the oncoming shift. At approximately the same time, this scene was repeated in many different stations throughout the city.

Fath Al-Haqr was something like an idiot savant. He wasn't the brightest, and he wasn't very articulate. But he had discovered a talent in himself, and had come to the attention of others. Today, he would use that talent until his task was ended and he was sent to Paradise. For now, he was moving along the street until he entered the Old Post Office Pavilion in downtown Washington. He was dressed in casually shabby clothes, with a few randomly applied paint smears on them. He carried a long case, similarly smeared, with a small briefcase in one hand. The bored looking security guard at the door glanced at him. "What's in there, buddy?:"

"I am a painter. I have very much liked the view from the Post Office tower, and I am to paint a cityscape from the observation deck."

"Let me see the case." Fath passed over the small case, which the guard opened and saw contained brushes, paints, rags, oils, and stuff he had no clue about, but looked sort of arty to him. "What's in the big one?" He gestured at the man's back.

"My easel and some clips, such things." He began to pull it off as a tour group got off their bus just behind him, with a group of school children. The guard made a resigned face.

"Go on, man. I gotta deal with all these kids." He made a shooing motion with his hand.

"Thank you, officer. If I have time later, maybe I can do a small portrait of you at work here, as a gift to your family?"

The guard gave him a half smile. "Thanks, man. We can talk about that later. Good luck with the painting."

"Oh, I believe I will execute a memorable work today." Fath gathered up his case and moved over to the elevator, pressing the button. The car arrived, and a young couple joined him for the ride up. They kept smiling at each other and murmuring, giggling. He dismissed them from his mind as he prepared himself.

The car reached the top, and the couple exited. Fath stepped out and looked around. As he had been told, there was one Park Police officer on the deck, who was now coming over to him.

"Hey, what are you doing up here with all that?" The officer asked.

"I am painting a cityscape. I have a permit, Officer." The man's voice was high pitched, almost shrilly annoying.

"I didn't know they gave permits for that up here." the officer said, wondering what idiot somewhere had given him permission to do this.

"Oh, yes." the man said. "I have special permission, let me show you." He reached his hand into one of the pockets of his cargo pants and came up with a small pistol. The officer's eyes went wide and he frantically grabbed for his holster. Fath calmly shot him several times, angling down into his lower belly and pelvis, where conventional body armor worn by law enforcement did not cover. The officer groaned and fell, bleeding heavily already. Fath calmly stepped forward and shot him once more in the throat. The gunshots echoed and the small crowd screamed. One man stepped towards him, and Fath shot him through the left eye. The man collapsed instantly, and the screams quieted, trailing off into whimpers. "I have no quarrel with you. If you people wish to live, simply leave. I suggest the stairs."

There was a small stampede as people fled. He waited, and the elevator came back up, with three more tourists who were greeted with his pistol in their faces. "Stairs. Leave. Now." He instructed them, sliding his paint case into the elevator part way to keep the door from closing. The three ran, the last one in line pausing to exchange a look and a nod with the shooter. Fath pulled a length of chain from his bag and locked the door at the top of the stairs with it and a simple padlock. He took the two dead bodies and used them to block the door, preventing the elevator from moving, and then retrieved his case from the elevator. He took the fallen officer's weapon, ammunition, and radio, as well as a few items from his briefcase. Fath paused as he heard a single gunshot echo up the stairs, and cries of fear about being pursued by the mad man with a gun. His accomplice, who had ridden up in the elevator with the two genuine tourists, had just shot out the light at the bottom of the stairs, as arranged previously. He then opened his easel case and threw out various thin metal struts and rags. Beneath them, he extracted the parts of his rifle, and quickly assembled it with the ease of long practice. As he listened to the first confused reports of trouble coming over the captured radio, he moved to one side of the observation deck and sighted down at the street. He let his glance play over the various figures, and selected a man in a blue suit. Slowly letting out his breath, he gently squeezed the trigger, and the man's head exploded in a shower of blood and bone. Screams echoed in the street, and he slowly shifted his rifle. Ah, excellent. A female police officer was running over to the fallen man, struggling to move quickly and also report on her radio. His shot took her through the chest, her body armor not designed to withstand the force of a specialized sniper rifle with hollow pointed rounds. He randomly selected a third target—a blonde woman in a business suit who was so wrapped up in her cell phone call she hadn't yet noted the chaos around her—and shot her, as well. Satisfied for the moment, he wandered to the other side of the platform. There were many targets yet, and he had time. They would block off the streets eventually, but that was fine. This was a fine sniper's nest for now.

Tina Lane sat at her desk and read the latest issue of Cosmo. She was bored. She was a technician at the major node that handled much of the phone traffic for the city. The system was well designed, and effortlessly handled the staggering volume of calls. However, since problems were rare, it left her without a lot to do. For some, this was a dream job, but for her it was frequently boring. She liked fixing things; it was why she had become a technician in the first place. Her thoughts drifted to looking into one of those online college courses or something. She blinked when the buzzer to the door sounded. No one ever came here. The supervisors only did inspections once a month or so, and they'd been through already. Since no one else was around at the moment, she went over and pressed the intercom. "Yes?"

"Delivery, pizza." The voice was slightly distorted by the speaker.

Tina paused. You weren't supposed to order to the place—it was supposed to be a secure facility—but sometimes people did. She wondered who the bonehead was this time, and then wondered if she could blackmail a slice or two in exchange for her silence. She just was not interested in the salad she'd brought in. Smiling at the thought, she opened the door. "Who's it for?" she asked.

There was a muffled sound, like a handclap, from under the box he held, and she fell backward, the silenced round neatly passing through her heart. The man stepped in and dropped the empty box on her body. There should be another few technicians around here somewhere. He just needed to deal with them and then take a hammer to the various machines here, and the city would start experiencing trouble with their phones almost at once, especially after events started unfolding and panicked calls were placed. The man pulled on a pair of glasses and picked up a clip board, playing the part of a bored auditor until he found his remaining targets. Such simple tasks as this were generally beneath him, but Nazzir had been well paid for this, and this portion, at least, he judged to be of minimal risk.

Wanda was practically glowing with excitement. Bernie had agreed to all her ideas, and she thought she had a few special additions that would make for some great visuals. Gina seemed to be a fun person to work with, and the shots she'd seen from her were really good. And now the two of them were down here by the bullpen, interviewing Hector Valdez, the star pitcher. Wanda had noticed the look between him and Gina, and decided she didn't want to know.

"Hector, thank you so much for talking with us. Could you tell us about the special event today?" Wanda was still somewhat amazed he had agreed to an interview so easily.

"As I understand, some of the Senators and Congressmen are playing a short game against each other for various charities. A few of us are on hand to watch and coach a bit before our game with Arizona."

"And are you rooting for one side or the other?" Wanda asked him with a smile.

"I don't fully understand the difference between the two groups. It's something I should be more interested in, but I admit I'm not. But then, I'm just a simple baseball player. I'm not a 'lechislator.' " Wanda had to try hard to not laugh out loud. Not only was she getting a great story, but her star interview was making fun of the idiot who'd passed up the chance to be here in the first place.

Wanda turned back to the camera, unable to fully hide her grin. "Well there we are. And good luck with the game, Hector." The camera light went out, and Gina lowered it.

Hector moved to speak with her just as Wanda heard some buzzing in her earpiece. "What was that?" She listened harder—someone had left a line open at the studio. It sounded like something big was breaking, but she couldn't hear what it was. Had someone said something about the Old Post Office?

Suliman bin Haqr had come to America and hoped to be rich, as most Americans seemed to be. He had found the "Land of Opportunity" was more like a land of conspiracy and prejudice, at least from what he'd seen. He got suspicious looks just from walking down the street in some places. After years of this, he'd soured on the entire "American Experience." He had considered going home, but a man had made contact and suggested he stay, that maybe someday there might be something he could do to show them how their poor treatment could rebound on them. In the meanwhile, he had finally made it through a special school and possessed a Commercial Driver's License. Then, a few months ago, he'd finally gotten the call he'd been waiting for. Today was his day! He would become a holy martyr and strike fear into the people who ignored him, jeered at him, went about their self absorbed little lives. He was coming up on his destination now.

Just south of Washington, DC, near the border of Alexandria City and Fairfax County, Interstates 395, 495, and 95 come together in a mess of merge lanes and snarled traffic. The location had been the home of legendary traffic tie-ups for years, and had finally been rebuilt. The new exchange featured soaring bridges and ramps, better merge areas, and similar improvements. It would be a stretch to say that traffic flowed smoothly, but the fiascos that had given the area nicknames like "the mixing bowl" and "Malfunction Junction" had at least greatly improved. The traffic was so thick here not only because of the heavy traffic around Washington, but because Route 95 was the major north-south route on the East Coast, linking Maine to Florida and all points in between. This was where Suliman was taking his tanker truck, freshly topped off with a load of fuel and then specially modified by some technicians loyal to the cause.

Anne Lifeld moved along in traffic, already thicker than she'd hoped. It was so damn hard to predict what the highways would be like around here on any given day. She sighed in frustration and pulled out her cell phone, hitting a number from speed dial. She frowned and waited through the voice mail message—Reggie really needed to shorten that, no matter how funny he thought he was. "Reg, it's me. I'm stuck on 95 again, and it's getting ugly early." She looked ahead and wondered what that idiot driving the truck was doing. Her mouth dropped open as she saw the truck smash a small hatch-back, crushing part of it and tossing it aside. The truck not only didn't slow, he was speeding up! What the hell was he thinking? She saw the truck destroy a guardrail, not even trying to slow, still going faster she thought. Too late, she realized it was going to drive straight into one of the columns that held up the overpass above her. The truck smashed into the support with a sound of tortured metal, and then it exploded like something out of one of the action movies Reggie kept making her watch. "Oh my God, Reggie." she managed to gasp out into the cell phone. The last thing she saw was the blossoming fireball that swept out to cover all the nearby cars and turn each into a small pyre for the drivers and passengers.

Omar had his own task to accomplish. He saw the driver smash his big rig into the concrete pillar and the resulting explosion. He wasn't sure how many died in the blast, but that actually wasn't the only goal. He'd been sitting across the way in the south bound lanes, pulled over with his hood up, for fifteen minutes, waiting for the truck. He stepped around the corner of his SUV, bringing his weapon up. A relic of the jihad against the Godless Russians in Afghanistan, this Stinger missile had also been modified. Omar fired and ran for his truck, having several other appointments to keep that day. No one had been sure if even the full tanker of fuel exploding and driving into the support would be enough. But, when you added a high explosive warhead slamming into the other side; well, that should do it. Omar got in just before the missile exploded. The already weakened pillar could not take the additional impact. With a horrifying shriek of collapsing concrete and twisting metal, it slowly, almost majestically, tumbled to the ground, some of it striking the roadway and adding to the fatalities. This would have been bad enough, but the loss of the support on a ramp overburdened by early rush hour traffic, coupled with the shockwaves of the two explosions, was simply too much. The fly-over ramp cracked and began falling, pieces raining down into the inferno below and then working back to the south side lanes, carrying more vehicles and their hapless occupants down dozens of feet. The rain of debris, cars, trucks, and other vehicles claimed many more lives, and shut down a major traffic point in the area. No one would drive this route for a very long time.

Finished, and aware that things were proceeding elsewhere, Nazzir took a few moments to leave a surprise for whoever would be sent to check on the call center. He worked easily and quickly, and completed his task. He left, checking his watch, and saw that he was slightly ahead of schedule. He imagined as the day progressed, it would be harder and harder to get around the city.

Wanda wrapped another small segment, an interview with some fans, and checked the time. "Ok, I think I have enough from down here for now. I'm going to go see about some of that other coverage I arranged. You coming?" she looked over at Gina.

The camerawoman paused, thinking. "No, I think I'm going to get some other shots down here. The regular crew's got that exhibition game covered, I'm going to try for some different shots."

Wanda nodded. "Ok, get us some good stuff. Catch you after the game."

By such random choices are fates sealed. These two would never meet again. One would die that afternoon, the other wondering later what the two of them should have done differently.

Officer Fakhoury arrived at the Old Post Office, seeing the emergency response units all over. He parked his cruiser and dove for the side of one of the armored Emergency Trucks. He saw he was next to Larry Joines, one of the SWAT specialists. "Hey, what's going." he looked closer and broke off "Are you ok?" The other officer, usually one of the toughest looking men around, looked pale, and was sweating profusely.

"Yeah....just don't feel too good. We gotta go take this guy out." Joines shivered and nearly threw up.

"You sure you're up for that?" The end of his question was lost when an officer moved between two vehicles and a loud boom echoed down the city street as the man was flung back in a spray of blood.

"SHIT!" Fakhoury cursed loudly. Medics started for the man and were held back by other officers.

Joines shook his head. "Bastard's just picking off who he wants. We had one team go set up to get him from a roof and he dropped the first one through the door. Fucker's good, give him that. We got a team trying to get a better look." He stiffened and then hurriedly turned his face shield up, spinning to the side as he retched violently.

Inside, the two men who had volunteered carefully opened the door at the base of the stairs. One was designated to report back on his throat mic in the quietest tones possible until they got closer, the other was looking for signs of the enemy. As they entered the landing area, they noted the light was out. Not wanting to advertise their location, they each activated the special night vision goggles they had been issued.

Gordon Hatch was a skilled spotter and observer, and had a lot of specialized training in various things that amounted to being sneaky and fighting dirty. Most days, he was one of the best around. Today, Gordon was feeling sick. In fact, his stomach kept cramping up and he was fighting off the feeling that he was about to puke all over the stairwell. He'd never live that down. Tom Ryder was creeping forward carefully, feeling faintly superior in one corner of his brain. He was an avid health food nut, and he knew his partner had chowed down on those free donuts earlier. Now, Gordon was moving slow, and Tom felt great. He decided not to say anything about it, trying to be generous. Both were somewhat distracted, and as the stairs wound around to the first landing, the light level dipped. The night vision goggles magnified available light, but there had to be light available. As a result, they both missed noticing the objects covering the landing floor. Right up until Gordon stepped on some of them, at least. The ball bearings shifted under his feet and sent him sprawling. His training would have been enough to break and even slightly quiet his fall, but as his arms instinctively slapped out, he drove the small spiked caltrops deep into his flesh and roared in pain. Caltrops were originally used against both infantry and cavalry, looking something like children's jacks, except the ends were as sharp as possible. When one stepped, or fell, on them, steel points were driven into the body part unlucky enough to make contact. These had been scattered about, along with the marbles, by Fath's accomplice as he had shot out the lights.

Up on the observation deck, Fath heard the noise, and moved to the doorway. He loosened the chain, picked up three specially prepared objects in sequence, and threw them down the stairs one after the other. He then quickly closed the doors and re-fastened them. Down below, Tom helped

Gordon up, or tried to. The sudden pain had finally broken his concentration, and Gordon barely managed to raise the face shield of his helmet in time before he threw up violently. His illness distracted them both, so they didn't see the incoming objects. The first was a simple flash-bang grenade, a device to incapacitate the enemy with concussion and bright light. It was tough to adapt to under normal circumstances. When one was wearing night vision gear, it was incredibly painful and devastating on the eyes. As both men howled and brought their hands up too late to cover their eyes and rub them, the next grenade made its presence known as the fragmentation device went off. A small explosion drove shards of metal all around the tiny confines of the stairway, several pieces managing to find their way past the body armor plates each SWAT officer was wearing. Fresh cries of pain were lost as the third device detonated, filling the stairs with a wash of flame.

Up above, Fath heard the pained sounds and the explosions, and moved to get a view downward. As he presumed, at least one of the men downstairs had been using their radio, and clearly his and his partner's anguished cries had been broadcast. Fath sighted in on one of the higher ranking officers who had unthinkingly risen as the hellish sounds came across the radio, and shot him at the socket joint of his right shoulder. Blood gouted everywhere as the man spun and fell, and Fath quickly re-aimed, catching the man who went to help the supervisor with a head-shot. With a few more fresh kills clouding their judgment, and the lower stairs burning away for a time, Fath thought he was safe enough for now. He wandered to the other side of the observation platform, but saw no targets exposed enough to warrant either the risk or the expenditure of ammunition. He was patient. He could wait. He knew he was going to die today, and it gave him a feeling of calm to know that he would soon be in Paradise. Down below, a rushed argument about the best way to handle the extraction of the two downed men came to an end when two more SWAT officers simply ignored the various shouted orders, went in, and pulled them out. Fath faintly heard the sounds, but didn't worry about it. He had more surprises in store for later.

Bernie Holt was at his desk at the station, listening to various news-feeds. Clearly something was wrong, but it was lots of small pieces of something, and some not so small. The details were still coming in about the disaster at the Mixing Bowl, with no one yet knowing how many deaths and millions in property damage. The sniper at the Old Post Office was apparently highly skilled, and was holding out fairly well so far. The cops were moving slowly, and seemed like they were having other problems. Scattered reports were coming in from all over about police looking horrible and/or throwing up all over the place. Certainly not every cop on duty, but quite a lot of them. He'd tried to get hold of a few of his reporters to call in extra people, but for some reason the phones seemed to be not working that well today. He had a feeling of dread settling in the pit of his stomach. Bernie was sure that something horrible was out there, and that as bad as all this had been, it was just going to get worse.

The Day Of

Things Get Worse

Gerry Franklin practically jumped out of his chair when his cell phone rang. He'd been sitting at his desk, his mind spinning, ever since Holmes and his team and left. How had it all gone this badly this fast? What should he have done different? What *COULD* he have done? He fumbled for his phone and finally got to it, opening it with a tired "Hello?"

"Agent Franklin, you sound exhausted. A rough few days, I would guess?" It was that voice again! The first one from years ago, the one that he'd tried so hard to forget.

"What do you want?" Franklin should be trying to trace the call, should be doing all manner of things, but he couldn't summon the energy.

"Why, I was simply checking on you. I do hope the police were not too problematic for a man of your skill at bending the truth. Were you able to keep your relationship with Agent Fowler from them?" The deep voice dripped with scorn and sarcasm, and Franklin winced at the images of Jill that flashed before his eyes again.

"Leave me alone, you bastard. What do you want from me?" his voice rasped into the phone.

"I wanted my brother back. But you kept him, knowing he was innocent. And then he was killed in prison. I wonder often if you had something to do with that, but I suppose it doesn't really matter." The voice went cold again then resumed its false friendliness. "I do hope you parted on good terms with your lovely wife and daughter this morning." he added.

For the first time in a while, Franklin felt something. Rage and fear coursed through him. "Stay away from my family. You have a problem with me, come find ME!" he practically shouted the last word into the phone.

"Why Agent Franklin, that sounds familiar. Now let me see where might I have heard something like that before? Ah yes, I recall. I told you something very similar several years ago I believe." The voice was maddeningly calm.

"My daughter's in school, and my wife's safe enough. I don't think even you are crazy enough to go after a whole school just to try and prove some point to me." Franklin was fighting hard to control his anger.

There was a deep sigh on the other end of the line. "Gerry, Gerry, I thought we understood each other. Of course I'd destroy an entire school, and kill every man, woman, and child there, if I needed to. But I don't. Have things really deteriorated that badly with your family? I know your long term affair with Agent Fowler hasn't been easy on them, but truly, are you at the point where I know more about what's happening with your family than you do?" There was a repeated tsk-tsk sound on the other end of the line.

"What are you talking about, you god-damn lunatic?" Franklin demanded.

"Language, please, Gerry. Let us attempt to remain professional. And do you really not know that it's Take Your Daughter To Work Day today? Have things truly deteriorated that badly between you, that I know your family's schedule better than you do? Marcie and Veronica should be," there was a pause, "why I believe they should be approximately at the Woodrow Wilson Bridge as we speak. I do hope that fares better than the so-called 'Mixing Bowl' did. Rather thoroughly mixed now, I would say."

"What are you." Franklin's voice trailed off.

"Oh, Gerry, are you that rattled already?" he asked in mock-distress. "Have you really not been paying attention? I do believe you should turn on the news. Your city is having a very bad day, and you're missing it. And after I went to all this trouble, too. Ah, well, perhaps I am a victim of my own success as the saying goes. Did the events with Conroy and Fowler and your rather pathetic brother shake you up so very much this early in the game?"

"My brother...he was...you did that, too?" Franklin half expected his earlier feeling of weakness to return, but instead felt a slow burning rage taking a greater hold of him.

"Oh, I think you will be surprised at what I can do over this next day or so. I cared very deeply for my brother, but as I studied your life, it didn't seem to me that you had a particular attachment to, well, much of anything I could discern. So I simply decided to target various things you seemed at least fond of. It sounds like I may have struck at least a few nerves. For now, do enjoy your day. Well, I suppose that's not very likely on reflection. Survive your day, and we'll speak again. Oh, and don't waste your effort, this disposable cell phone is going in the trash in just a moment. Farewell for now." He abruptly hung up.

Franklin cursed as he tried to figure out what to do next. Zeroing in on a portion of the conversation, he picked up his phone and dialed his daughter's cell phone. Maddeningly, all he got for his efforts was a "your call can not be completed as dialed" message. Cursing, he turned to his computer and brought up a local news site, trying to catch up on what was occurring, occasionally hitting redial and getting nowhere as he tried to contact his daughter.

The Northwest section of Washington, DC, is one of the wealthier areas of the city. Many fine homes are located here, some upscale businesses, several embassies and chanceries, and American University. When the cell phone tower was first being constructed here, it was the subject of much resistance and even several lawsuits. Eventually, the tower was built, despite all the protests.

Many people have commented on, and profited by, the maxim that if you look like you know what you're doing, no one will question you. So, rather than attempting some stealthy, guerrilla like approach, the beat up silver work van pulled up in front of the tower very openly and parked there. A man dressed in coveralls got out, walked up to the gate, and soon had it open. If no one noticed his picking the lock rather than opening it with a key, or his leaving a few bundles around the tower rather than performing any actual repairs, no one could blame the neighbors. So far that day, a major highway had been destroyed and a sniper was picking off targets with a terrifying ease downtown. The man locked the gate behind him and left, driving off in his van. Ten minutes after his unnoticed departure, in a carefully worked out sequence, the bundles detonated. The echoes of the explosions were lost in the sounds of tortured metal giving way, and the towering structure toppled. It would have been easy enough to arrange for it to drop straight down, but that wasn't really the idea behind most of these acts. The pylon of steel fell, crushing a restaurant, several parked cars, and demolishing part of a small office building on the way down. It also happened to catch a commuter van full of tired office workers, many of whom were anxiously trying to reach loved ones in the wake of the shootings and the calamity on the highway. The van was crushed, and all told, the debris blocked a good bit of Wisconsin Avenue, another major way in and out of the District. Almost unnoticed in the carnage, a major choke point for cell phone traffic in the city was destroyed. The body count would reach the mid-double digits by the end of the day, with many more injured. And the day was far from over.

Marcie Franklin was tired, but fairly happy, a somewhat rare event these days. Her official job title was "office manager" for a small law firm in Maryland, but in actuality, she pretty much ran the business. Of course, when there was any kind of dispute or disagreement, the actual attorney with his name on the door held sway, but that was an unusual occurrence. Marcie handled the day to day running of the office, the investigators, paralegals, and the myriad details that went into keeping the business solvent. The attorney, Gene Carstone, handled the court appearances and the negotiations with opposing counsel. At times, during the once-monthly or so group lunches he bought for everyone, he likened her to a squire to his knight. She thought that was a bit egotistical on his part, but fairly accurate as far as it went.

Marcie looked over at her daughter, who sat in the passenger seat, leaning back, eyes closed. She was sure she wasn't actually asleep. The older woman looked back at the road, driving down Indian Head Highway as they neared the Beltway. "So, what'd you think?"

Veronica didn't react for a minute, and then leaned forward, opening her eyes. "I think you're really good at what you do, Mom. You have that whole place down perfect."

Marcie waited, gauging the voice. "But.?" she asked after a moment.

"But it's really not something I want to do, Mom." Veronica looked nervously over at her. "No offense."

Marcie laughed. "Hon, this wasn't 'I'm going to tell you what to do with your life.' This was more showing you what I do with mine, at work anyway."

"So, it's ok I don't want to go work in an office?" Veronica looked back at her, smiling with a mixture of shyness and self-consciousness and nervousness.

Marcie spared her daughter a quick look, hurriedly returning her eyes to the traffic. "No one says you have to work in an office. Lots of people don't. Now, I know you don't like talking about this, but I'm going to for a minute." She looked at her again. "You're a very smart girl. You have options that neither your father nor I did. You can do almost anything you want, I think. That's something you're going to have to decide. We'll both help you however we can, but at the end of day, you have to live your life. So no, I'm not going to tell you how to do that."

There was another long pause, and Marcie frowned. Traffic seemed hideous, much worse than normal. Since they had very different tastes in music, mother and daughter had long ago agreed not to listen to the radio in the car, so as usual for them, it was off. In the office, Marcie was too busy, and when Veronica hadn't been being shown how various parts of the business worked, she'd had on her iPod, so neither one had actually heard about the various tragic events taking place that day.

"Mom...can I ask you something?" Veronica ventured after a few more moments.

'Uh-oh' a voice in Marcie's head said. This could be nearly anything from her wildly unpredictable, precocious daughter. "What is it, Ronnie?" she asked, a trifle warily.

"How bad are things between you and Dad?" Veronica's voice was low, but the words carried clearly. The silence thickened for a few minutes, and Veronica finally ventured "That bad, huh?"

"Why do you ask, hon?" Marcie was impressed with herself, that she managed to keep her voice level.

"I'm sixteen, I'm not stupid. I know you two aren't getting along that well, I just don't know how bad it is. I can see it when you're with each other, trying to pretend it's all ok, I guess for me? Or maybe because you're not admitting it to yourselves? But you never touch each other, you talk about things, but you never really talk, y'know?" The girl paused. "Is one of you having an affair or something?"

Marcie was stunned by her daughter's words. She tried to frame a response, glancing over at her and then back at the truly horrendous traffic. "Honey...it's not that simple." She felt the girl's eyes on her, and the weight of the gaze was like a slap.

One of the few things Marcie and Gerry still talked about at length was Veronica. They both agreed that she was incredibly smart and perceptive, and seemed to possess an amazing wisdom and insight. They had both long ago started diverting a large amount of their incomes, as much as they could spare, maybe a bit more at times, into a college fund for her so she could go wherever she wanted. It seemed inevitable she would decide to go, she simply enjoyed learning new things too much. Marcie, unfortunately for her, was about to be on the receiving end of another flash of her girl's insight. "Oh my God, you both are." There was hurt and disbelief in her voice as she stared accusingly at her mother. "Who is it, Mom? Is it Gene? Your boss?" She studied her face closely and Marcie felt annoyance.

"It doesn't matter, hon. Your Dad and I, we haven't been what you would call close in years. And I got, well, lonely." She realized how pathetic that must sound to her daughter, and willed herself to shut up.

Veronica threw herself backward in her seat, arms folded. "You got lonely. So you started an affair with your boss? Cliché much, Mom?" There was pain in her voice, which Marcie wished wasn't there.

"I didn't say I started it," she began.

"I met him, remember? He's clueless. Brilliant; I bet he's amazing in court," Marcie let out a mental sigh of relief she hadn't said "in bed." Veronica continued, "but personal stuff? You made the first moves." It was said flatly, no hesitation, no uncertainty. Marcie had said not long ago, only mostly in jest, that she thought Veronica would clean up on the professional poker circuit. The thought came to her again and she pushed it aside, knowing she was trying to distract herself.

Veronica went on. "So why are you two even still togeth-" she broke off. "Me. You're still together because of me, because you think it's better for me. So you're not happy, you're both cheating, and this is better? Better than what?" She flung out the last word, her voice rising in despair and pain, and Marcie wished she *was* almost anywhere else, and wondered in passing what else could go wrong today.

The bomb that destroyed the Alfred P. Murrah Federal Building in Oklahoma City terrified many people. The act itself, of course, scared the residents of the city, and the country in general, making them wonder if the place they worked, or shopped, or left their kids in day care, would be next. It caused great concern to law enforcement and government agencies because the ingredients to make it were not really all that hard to get, and rental trucks were available everywhere. True, watch lists and computer programs had been set up to try and catch suspicious purchases, but they were easy enough to hide, or at least disperse, among several different purchases by different buyers—or at least men with different identification in different places.

The device carefully prepared for this day and its special target was a refinement on that earlier bomb. This truck had been stolen, its license plates swapped out with others, and very special modifications made to the cargo area. The roof had been reinforced with thick metal plating, welded carefully together. It wasn't a pretty job, but it didn't need to be. It just needed to hold. The truck was then loaded with the components required to create the desired blast. These men were not dedicated believers to the cause. They would park their vessels of destruction and then flee. What the drivers did not know was that they were not alone—there were four such trucks with special instructions on exactly where to park. Further, the detonators that the drivers had been given were useless. They would be set off by a spotter who had been instructed to blow them in a special sequence, but not until a certain car was on the bridge.

Woodrow Wilson had been the 28th President of the

United States. He had worked hard to lead the country during the Great War, as it was called then, or World War I, as it's more commonly known now. It was perhaps unfair to his legacy that in the Washington area, his name was best known for the bridge that bore his name. The Wilson Bridge spans the Potomac River between Maryland and Virginia, and is the frequent scene of all manner of traffic tie ups. It was on to this bridge, slowly, inch by inch, that Marcie Franklin maneuvered her car. The traffic, much worse than she had ever seen, had her vaguely curious, but the conversation with Veronica was clearly important, and she couldn't think of a good way to say "Hon, hold that thought while I turn on the radio and see what's going on, ok?"

Veronica had been firing off questions that Marcie either could not answer or didn't want to, and showed no signs of stopping. "Ok, I'm still trying to get a handle on all this. Do you know who it is that Dad's...seeing?" She was clearly groping for the right words in this emotional minefield.

"It's not something we've talked about." Marcie answered, thinking that it was more like they'd both pretended not to know. She noticed a truck pulled over to the side of the road, and a man getting out and suddenly running back along the bridge.

"But you're sure he's with someone, and you are too. And you're not happy, either of you." She shook her head. "But somehow you both think this is a good idea?"

"There's a lot to it, it's not just that simple. And we don't hate each other, we're just used to each other." Marcie was wondering which one of them was the parent here. "It's easier."

"Easier and used to each other?" Veronica shook her head. "Those are reasons to stay together?" Whatever Marcie's reply would have been, it was lost in a loud CRUMP! of detonation behind them. "Mom? What was that?" Marcie started to answer when there was a sickening lurch under them.

The Wilson Bridge is the site of traffic snarls for several different reasons. Many crossing over it slow down, either to admire the view or from a fear of heights. Sometimes severe winds make some drivers cautious. And occasionally there is a large boat that requires passage. To make sure such vessels can get through, the Woodrow Wilson bridge is a drawbridge. When the trucks were placed and then set off, each explosion was on a part of the huge hinge mechanism that allowed the bridge to be raised. The shockwaves rippled through the surface of the bridge, and it buckled, the anchors that connected the bridge to the riverbank giving way. There was a scream of tortured metal, and cars began sliding towards the chasms developing in the roadway. Veronica Franklin felt their car sliding backward and screamed, and then everything went black.

Word of the calamitous events around the city was spreading, of course. The news was traveling slower than one would expect—but then in addition to the obvious issues plaguing the Capitol City, people were noticing major problems with both the conventional telephones and their various cells. This was, in turn, causing even more anxiety. The officials at Nationals Park had debated for a time, but finally decided to go ahead with the game as scheduled. The exhibition with the Senators vs. the Congressmen had been played out, and certainly provided enough humor for the various sports shows that liked to feature bloopers and such things. The event had been a moderate success, with the Senators eking out a one-run victory.

Wanda had done a few fan reactions, and even gotten a short interview with Senator James Metcalfe of South Dakota, the team captain. He looked happy, if tired, and kept his remarks gracious and short. "We all played hard, and the important thing is that the National After School Sports Association got some good donations and press time. They're a great cause, providing sports equipment in school districts where there just isn't the budget for it."

Wanda had managed to get her interview back after a few minutes more of what sounded like a Public Relations sound-bite, and wished the Senator luck if he played again next year. There was already talk of making it an annual event. The cameraman, Jim Lopresti, had shot the exchange competently, but not as well as Gina would have, Wanda thought. Gina was wandering around getting more shots of the Park as the Nationals and Diamondbacks prepared for their actual game. Several of the lawmakers had found various excuses to stay and take in the game, probably why some of them agreed to play in the first place, a cynical person may have thought. Looking down at her watch, Wanda realized she had little time, and she hurried out of the Park, and to a nearby empty parking lot. She had gotten special permission for this as soon as she learned the game was hers to cover. It'd taken several favors being called in, and one well placed bribe, of a sort. Feminine wiles were all well and good, but never underestimated the power of tickets on the fifty yard line for a Washington Redskins home game. Getting those tickets time to time had been one of her best investments, and, pricey though they were, they had proven well worth it. Things were tense with the various strange accidents and the sniper loose at the Pavilion, but the chopper usually used for traffic coverage was still waiting for her, Mike Harrington waiting in the pilot's seat. She got in, fastened the various safety belts, and donned the headset. "All set?" he asked, and she flashed a smile and thumbs up.

Wanda was a tiny bit afraid of heights, a fact she concealed from most and had worked to overcome in her time as a traffic reporter. She was all right when actually flying now, but the take off still rattled her badly, so she closed her eyes and tried to think calm thoughts as Mike spun up the rotors and took them up into a tight arc over Nationals Park.

After a few moments, Mike said "It's ok, we're up, and about where you wanted us." Wanda opened her eyes and looked down, smiling. Sure, there had been footage shot from blimps and such before, but this was a bit different, and it had been a while since anyone had done this. Plus, with it being such a nice, clear day, the framing was perfect, and the system that usually provided images for the traffic reports would cover this perfectly.

Their timing was great and the Nationals were taking the field. Wanda, while no expert, had gotten adept at using the cameras in the chopper. She zoomed around, setting up shots of the various players. She lingered longest on Cliff Tremayne, the first baseman, who had a decent batting average and she thought was damn cute, and of course Hector Valdez. The pitcher was warming up, throwing to Haynes, the catcher, and starting to build up the speed in his pitches. His fastball was a rightly feared weapon in the Nats' arsenal. She couldn't blame Gina for what she was pretty sure had happened—Hector was a good looking man, clearly in great shape, and seemed like he had a lot of energy. Wanda wondered briefly what he'd be like in bed, but then pushed the thoughts aside, both because of wanting to do her job as well as she could, and because of her budding friendship with Gina, which she didn't want to screw up. She was jarred suddenly when Mike, who was noted for going whole flights without a word, suddenly said "What the hell?" and banked them hard left.

Ammar Hadad's plan was far reaching and multi faceted. He'd had years to put it together, spent a staggering amount of money, and blended many different elements. There were the general strikes on the city, and interlaced with them, his own more personally targeted agenda. The destruction of the highway interchange had panicked many, and the damage to the communications lines in the city was furthering that. The sniper, Fath, had diverted much of the city's emergency response attention, and the poisoned pastries were doing well. Not everyone who ate them would die, of course. Dosages varied by body weight, metabolism, and how many the victim ate. There were several more surprises yet to come, but this one would instantly sweep the country. Using a rented warehouse and several shipments of the disassembled parts, the special group had rebuilt a third-hand, beat up, old Huey helicopter. They had mounted several guns, and then added a special cargo. Some had been worried about the parts getting in to the country, but security at the various cargo ports was laughable, and the huge shipping containers were simply too numerous for all of them to be searched. With everything readied, they had brought in a special consultant for their next step. The man, a disgruntled ex-Army engineer, had been hired to plant charges in a specified sequence, and been told the desired result. He had gone over the plans, made a few of his own refinements, and completed the task. He'd been paid half up front, as he insisted, but they'd saved the second half of his fee when they killed him as soon as he said he was done. Budget savings and tighter security, a great combination.

Abdul Hamid was proud to have been given this special task. His experience against the Russian Army in the 80's had hardened his skills and resolve, and he was very much a believer in the Prophet Mohammed, Peace be upon Him. Everyone was in the chopper, and he turned to his second, Misbah. "Let us see if the money we paid that fool was well spent." He held up a remote detonator and pressed the button. A series of explosions rocked the warehouse, virtually destroying the building, and great deal around it, and blowing the roof off and aside. With a deft touch on the controls, Misbah guided them up and out of the wreckage. They'd manage to inflict a good bit of damage on the neighborhood, but that was secondary. They headed toward their target, and prepared themselves. The heavily laden, old, and worn out aircraft wasn't the most graceful thing in the skies, but it didn't need to be. It simply needed to take them to their destination and hold them aloft long enough to wreak some havoc. Misbah cursed suddenly as they popped up over the walls of the Park and suddenly found themselves far too close to a news helicopter. Both pilots banked in opposite directions, to the sudden displeasure, and mild nausea, of their respective occupants.

Mazin bin Hakkad checked his heavy weapon for the final time. He was most ready to make his journey to Paradise, and was thrilled to be sending some of these lazy, godless Americans to Sheol first. He lurched as Misbah curved the chopper suddenly, and nearly opened fire early, but managed to not pull the trigger all the way back. He smiled and started lining up the weapon on the stands.

Hector was in a great mood. The charity event had gone well, and he was very much in favor of getting sports equipment to underprivileged schools. It was a good day, he was on the mound, and last night had gone well. Seeing Gina again today had been nice actually, no feelings of her pressuring him, but her smiling at him in a friendly way—this was a great thing to him. He frowned as he looked up. What in the hell was that idiot in the helicopter doing?

Gina had used her press pass to get a decent spot for herself and her gear, and set everything up. She was recording her shots, and sending them out on the closed circuit in the Park, as well as on a special back up straight to the studio. Gina had gotten some very good shots during the charity game, and things hadn't been all weird with Hector. She smiled to herself at that. Her smile faded as her attention was diverted upwards—that wasn't Wanda's chopper doing something stupid, was it?

Officer Jon LaSalle was having a bizarre day. It had started off well enough, and he'd gotten to the Park in plenty of time, arriving for the early briefing and roll call. Then he'd been hearing throughout the day about the sniper, and cops falling out all over the city, all sickened by something or other. He, along with several others here on overtime, had volunteered to leave and respond to the various other disasters, but were being told so far to stay put. He was frustrated, but would do what he was told. A new sound made him glance upward, and he saw an old, military surplus-looking helicopter come perilously close to a news helicopter. What the hell was THAT about?

Mazin steadied himself, and then slowly turned the gun. Lining up on the stands, he waited, and when Abdul Hamid gave the order, he pulled the trigger. Rounds raced out of the weapon and began stitching across the spectators. Shock prevented them from moving at first, then cries of pain spurred them into motion. He traversed the gun barrel and followed the crowd as they panicked, fled, and started turning into a stampede.

LaSalle saw the crowd surging forward, the helicopter, unbelievably, firing on them like something out of a war movie, and his training and experience kicked in. He moved quickly up the aisle, away from the lower sections where the near-mob was gathering. LaSalle knew some of them would be hurt, even killed, by the out of control running, but he also knew that he had no way of stopping them. Trying to block them out, he moved inward along the row of seats, taking himself farther from the crowd, his pistol out without his remembering drawing it. He crouched down behind some seats, steadied the barrel on the seat back in front of him, drew in a deep breath, released it slowly, and began firing.

A pistol is not a weapon designed for long range. Hitting something at 25 yards is considered a respectable shot, and the furthest many law enforcement officers are trained to. Also, LaSalle, while making qualification easily each time he was tested, was not a top marksman. But people were dying, and he had to try something. He fired knowing his odds of hitting anything important were minimal at best, and that the stopping power of the pistol was negligible against something like the chopper.

Wanda was almost dazed, amazed this was happening right in front of her. Her fingers automatically worked the camera controls, and the shot came out better than she had any right to hope. The one brave officer, standing his ground, trying to protect his people. She breathed a silent prayer for him as she began composing a report in her head, her free hand fumbling for her cell phone.

Misbah flinched and let out a stream of curses in Farsi. Over the headsets, he yelled out "That fool is shooting at us and hitting us! Take care of him!" The chopper flight smoothed out as Mazid recovered from the shock of seeing two small holes punched in the canopy of the cockpit. Mazin began swinging his gun around, rounds chewing up the now empty plastic seats, fire tracking back towards LaSalle.

Gina kept her camera on Hector. It wasn't personal interest; she just had a feeling. He'd ducked initially, as did almost everyone, as the gunfire began blasting out. Then, while most of the players were running for the doors off the field, she saw him straighten up, a look of mingled resolve and rage on his face. He stretched his arm, unnoticed by the combatants, and then did the impossible.

Hector was livid. These were his fans. They were here to see him, and now they were in danger because of that. These people let him do what he lived for. This would not happen. Not while he breathed. With every bit of focus, control, and power at his command, he threw the best and most important pitch of his life.

When the chaos of this horrible day died, and the innumerable and inevitable news reports and specials were shown about it, some images would become almost as iconic as the firefighters draping the huge flag over the Pentagon wall several years ago. Some of them would be of Officer

LaSalle and the gunfight he got into knowing he couldn't win it. But one of the most repeated pieces of footage would be what Gina shot as Hector, throwing straight up, against the wash of the chopper blades, fired off a fastball that any major leaguer on the best day of his career simply wouldn't have been able to hit. It was just the perfect pitch. Unprepared, taken wholly by surprise, Mazin was just about to finally silence that annoying policeman when his jaw was broken by the impact of an expertly thrown baseball. Striking harder than a punch from a heavy weight champ, the impact knocked him out as his jaw shattered, and he fell. Some parts hadn't been installed in the rebuilt helicopter, and the gunner safety belts were among them. Mazin plummeted through the air and crashed onto the field, somewhere near second base. The gun fell silent and there was a moment of shock from everyone left who witnessed it. Abdul could not keep the shocked expression from his face as he stared for a moment, then yelled at Misbah "Take us down!" Misbah nodded grimly and dove.

Hector was reaching for another ball when he heard the change in engine pitch. He ran quickly to the side, Gina chanting "Get out of there, get out of there" under her breath, not that anyone could have heard her. Gina's camera was plugged into the feed back to the studio, and as Wanda finally made contact, yelling at an already somewhat overwhelmed Bernie "Check the feed from the Park! NOW!" Wanda made sure her own camera was sending as well. Bernie raced to the studio, calling for them to bring up the images from Wanda and Gina's cameras.

Misbah brought them down lower and lower, Hector racing away from them, wondering if he was about to be shot in the back for his efforts. LaSalle, stunned for a moment by the throw, muttered "Son of a bitch" and began firing again, spent shells tinkling down onto the concrete around him. Abdul waited until the craft was roughly six feet off the in-field, and then cried out "God is most great!" and pressed the button on the control tightly clenched in his hand.

A great deal of care had gone into the preparation of this payload. Several types of explosives had been used. The goals here were different than those of many of the blasts triggered that day. This one was to do the most damage possible to much more fragile targets than concrete, steel, or vehicles. The blast utterly annihilated the helicopter, and a wave of fire rushed out in all directions. It scorched the carefully tended grass of the field, and reduced Hector to burnt wreckage in seconds. The blast wave of fire carried outward, reaching Gina next as she and her camera both effectively melted in the onslaught. LaSalle had a moment to blurt out half a profanity before the fire swept over him, and those who hadn't been fortunate enough to get far enough away, down the ramps and stairs of the park. Several Senators and Congressmen were among those who perished in the firestorm as the Park's own shape helped propel the inferno along the hallways. Bernie, back at the studio, said a prayer he would have sworn he didn't remember if asked, from his days as a youth at Temple. Wanda and Mike were thrown violently to the side by the blast-wave, as Mike waged a grim battle with the controls. After endless seconds when both were convinced they would be added to the fatalities at the Park, he got the ship flying level. Wanda felt the tears running down her face as Bernie asked her if she was still there, if she was ok, his voice sounding impossibly far away on the cell phone.

Now events were speeding forward even faster. The images from the game reached a nationwide audience, some of whom had only just been starting to learn of the strikes in DC. Stunned fans nationwide blinked at their screens in disbelief. People who lived or worked near Nationals Park ran into the street, and mistook the blast cloud, starting a rumor that the field had been nuked. More people began making frantic phone calls to friends and relatives in Washington, further overloading the stressed and damaged telephone circuits. The death toll jumped up hugely from the blast at the park, and the many who were killed by the stampeding fans. Emergency response was slow, already stretched thin by the earlier events of the day. And Ammar Hadad wasn't done with the nation's capitol yet.

Like many cities, Washington, DC, has a well developed public transportation system. It certainly has its flaws, as many commuters would rather grumpily tell you at the end of a day filled with delays in their trips. The Metro system, as the trains were called, traveled through various tunnels and over different bridges. The different lines were color coded, with each one covering different areas. The Yellow Line traveled out of Washington into Virginia, passing the Pentagon, the mall at Crystal City, and various other points of interest before moving into the suburbs of Northern Virginia. What made the Yellow Line of particular interest to Hadad was that it did not cross the Potomac River on a bridge—it traveled under the water in a submerged tunnel.

Panic was well and truly sweeping the city. The highways were exploding, cell towers were falling, there was a sniper on the loose, and now Nationals Park had been hit. People were fleeing the city, and the often crowded Metro trains were filled near to bursting. People exchanged rumors, each more incredible than the last. In the last car of this Yellow Line train, Nasser bin Wasid silently prayed. He had been recruited and given the honor of becoming a martyr some time ago, and was ready. He counted down silently, as he'd been trained, from the time the train had left L'Enfant Plaza, the last station in Washington, DC. By his figuring, he must be roughly in the middle of the tunnel. He set off the powerful explosives under his jacket, shredding the rail car and killing the people packed in around him. He was not alone on this train however. Wasim in the first car followed suit a moment later, bringing the train to a screeching halt and killing even more. The two blasts and the impact of the wrecked train echoed throughout the tunnel. The moaning survivors tried to figure out what had happened, their cries of pain and fear drowning out a more ominous sound. While built strongly and with care, the tunnel had not been designed to withstand such stresses. The ceiling creaked and groaned, as a tiny crack spread, and grew wider, and spawned more.

Linda Gant slowly pushed herself to her feet. Her head was ringing, and she wiped blood from her nose. She wasn't sure what had just happened to her train, but she was pretty sure it was connected to everything else she'd been hearing about. She'd had some first aid classes at work and was a generally helpful person, caring for others. She began slowly and methodically checking the people nearest her, assessing the extent of their injuries, and sorrowfully turning away from the ones that were in the arms of whatever God they had believed in. She was bandaging the arm of a somewhat older man who was trying to hold still when she heard something hitting the roof of the car. She hoped it was some kind of rescuers with first aid supplies—she could only do so much with ripped up sleeves and the like. The tapping became a thudding, and then a steady roar as the ceiling gave way and water poured in. Those who weren't smashed flat and crushed soon had to deal with the rapidly rising water level. Their screams echoed down the darkened, smoky tunnel.

Ariel looked at her screen glumly. She'd been receiving a steady stream of information, all of it bad. The sniper had been just the tip of the iceberg, and she was still collecting information. "Ok, we've got the two dead last night, they've blown up the Mixing Bowl, the Wilson's been hit, and they fire bombed Nationals Park. And I doubt they're done."

Holmes shook his head, his dark skin a bit ashen looking at the reports of carnage coming in. "All right, we need to figure out what's going on, what their plan is, see if we can get ahead of this. From what we got out of Franklin, it sounds like this all goes back to when he busted Hadad. What can you find out about him, Ariel?"

She'd been pulling up that data before all the news had begun hitting. She went back to the other window on her laptop. "Fadi Hadad, reported to be one of the major bank rollers of several factions of Al-Qaeda, and a few others. Franklin led the investigation that zeroed in on him, looks like he did some solid research there. But there're some holes, too. I'm not sure he did all this…anyway, Franklin and his team got him, and it does kind of sound like he confessed. He certainly didn't deny any of it."

Holmes looked over at her, shutting out the events of the day, focusing on unraveling the motive behind them. "Where is he? Can we get someone to talk to him for us?"

She scrolled down further and frowned. "Only if you have a Ouija board. Looks like he got killed. He was waiting for a transport to a court hearing, and someone fucked up hard and put him in with a bunch of other prisoners. They beat him to death when they figured out who he was."

"Well…shit." Holmes swore rarely, but Ariel couldn't blame him. "Ok, so that's not going to get us anywhere. What did he have for family, or friends who'd care enough to set all this up?"

Ariel punched through more records on her keyboard. "Not much. It doesn't seem like he was really close with too many people. His family…" she trailed off.

"His family what?" Holmes asked again. In the far corner of the room, Craigson was making calls on his cell phone, trying to get more information on what was happening in the city.

"Well…it says they were reported killed, but something doesn't look right here. I think someone's been playing with the records." Ariel looked more intently at her screen. "I can probably dig it out if I have a while."

"I don't think we have a while, Ariel." Holmes said, his voice serious.

She shrugged and looked at him helplessly. "What do you want me to do? I can't just wave my hands and make the information show up."

"If you think the files were doctored, we probably know who did it. Who's the most tied in to this mess?" Holmes looked back at her.

"Back to Franklin again?" she asked.

"Unless you have a better idea," Holmes countered.

Craigson walked over, hanging up. "Sounds like something just blew up in one of the Metro tunnels, too. We need to do something here."

Holmes led them out of his commandeered conference room with a determined expression on his face. He would not be accepting any evasions now, nor take any pity on the man. There was simply too much at stake now.

Rafe Segovia was living a nightmare. No, he'd had his share of nightmares over the years, and this was far worse. Notionally, it was his day off, but he had agreed to come in and work the always under-staffed communications center for a shift. He'd been one of the ones in the best position to first see the scope of what was happening. Rafe had access to various security cameras, and the calls from the public, and the radio chatter among his fellow officers. He could feel his stomach churning as had heard the first "Officer Down!" calls from the Post Office Pavilion, and listened as that situation got worse and worse. They still didn't have the damn sniper; he was forted up tight up on the deck and had proven to be an amazingly skilled shot. Then the reports had flooded in on the mutual assistance calls for the hell that had erupted on the highway, with the new Mixing Bowl ramp collapsing, and reports of a truck bomb that set it off, then the Wilson being attacked. As usual, in case things got slow, there was a television playing in the background, and everyone in the call center had watched, horror-struck, as the strange helicopter had attacked the Nats game, cheered when Valdez made that amazing throw to take out the gunner, then gone more or less numb when the field had vanished under a wave of fire.

Rafe sat at his console, stunned, his usually agile brain shocked into uselessly spinning its wheels. Everyone was being pulled in too many directions at once—no one had a plan covering something this bad, with this many hits in different places. He knew that the sniper should have been taken by now, but he was clearly not negotiating and the police were spread thin, especially with was whatever was making so many of them so damn sick. Rafe hadn't been at any of the roll calls today, so he was unaware of the donuts being given out, and most of the ones who did know about them were too busy either trying not to be shot, helping the civilians they could still get to, or just plain throwing up (or worse) to put it together. He listened as the preparations were being made to try and simply storm the tower. That was about the last choice, but they couldn't just sit on him and contain him with so much else demanding manpower elsewhere. SWAT had made up their somewhat depleted ranks by drafting a few of the officers that weren't sickened and giving them a crash course in what was expected, mostly consisting of "Hold this, give it to me when I tell you, and if you see this asshole, SHOOT HIM."

A familiar voice caught Rafe's attention as they checked the equipment for the SWAT unit preparing to try and take the tower. Rafe pulled his mic back down and said "Dispatch to SWAT 5-b, roll to channel 5."

He adjusted his own settings, and waited, almost at once hearing "SWAT 5-b on Channel 5, go."

"What's Rafe's Rule #1?" he asked, trying for a light tone.

" 'Never volunteer.' I know, I know. But it's a mess out here, and they need whoever they can get that shoots straight and isn't throwing up everywhere. It's bad, Rafe. It's really bad." Farris' voice lowered on those last few words.

"Well, kid, I can't fault your enthusiasm, and it doesn't sound like I could, or should, talk you out of it. Just…keep your damn head down, ok?" Rafe wondered when he had started sounding like someone's parent.

Apparently Farris picked up on the same feeling, as he said "Ok, Dad," in a somewhat mocking voice.

"Keep it up, kid, and you're grounded. Now go get this asshole. Back to tac channel." He dialed back to the main channel for this operation and listened to the preparations underway. Nothing ever went smoothly—a friend of his said often "No plan survives initial contact with the enemy"—but it sounded like they had as much covered as they could.

There were many obstacles confronting the assault team. Some they could plan for, and some members of the team had been doing just that since the first "Officer down" call. The building being run by the Federal Government had some pluses, for example the blueprints being up to date, thorough, and easily available. Less convenient was the Park Police command presence on scene. There had been some bickering back and forth, tempers running high as both agencies had lost people in this incident, until the DC Police Captain finally asked, "So we give this to you—then what? You have SWAT? You have a way to take the place? Assault training?" After much glowering at each other, Park Police ceded command to DC Metro, who had all their elements on scene already and were clearly ready and eager to go.

The first thing they were trying to overcome were the marbles and caltrops littering the first landing. After listening to various debates about magnets, shop-vacs, and other such plans, one of the officers searched around until he found one of the janitorial staff, and asked a simple question, "Hey, buddy, you got a broom?" With a few men moving very carefully forward first, holding ballistic shields and ready to dive for cover should more grenades make an appearance, Officer Young used long strokes of a simple push broom to clear the devices from the landing. The first few stairs had been covered with towels, so there was not even a clinking of falling metal to reveal their position.

Unfortunately, there were not a lot of options. The very simplicity of the design here worked against them. They had finally decided on a three part plan, each segment with its difficulties, and simply acknowledged they had been dealt a crappy hand and would have to play it.

Atop the tower, Fath knew he was running out of time. It had been quite a while since a target had presented itself to him, and things had gotten quiet. He was certain that they had come up with some sort of plan of attack, and would be coming soon. Fine, he was ready. Insha'Allah, he would bring a few more down before he was taken to Paradise. He cautiously peered over one of the railings, his eye sweeping for another opportunity, or at least a hint of what was to come.

Everyone was as ready as they could be. Equipment was checked a final time, radios tested, straps tightened. Everything came up ready. Rick Grant, the overall tactical commander, finally drew in a deep breath and gave a double click on his radio mic. It was time to go.

On several surrounding buildings, small units burst out of various stairwells on to the roofs. Aiming as best they could for a target they couldn't really see, they fired short bursts up at the observation deck. Even Fath, resolved to die in his undertaking, was surprised by the ferocity of the fire and flinched back. The group at the bottom of the stairs swept forward, moving as quickly, but quietly, as possible. As soon as they were on the final leg of stairs that led straight up to the deck, they began firing various specialized weapons. A pepper-ball gun was one of the first—like the weapons used in war games that fired balls of paint, only these projectiles were filled with pepper gas, a powerful agent that made those nearby not protected by gas masks cough, choke, and gasp. Another launcher sent a few flash-bang grenades arcing upward, similar to the ones Fath himself had used on the first SWAT officers in the stairwell. The rest had assault rifles at the ready, and were simply waiting for a target.

The third prong of the attack revolved around one of the team's unique assets. Walt Milan could have made a fortune in the movie special effects business, and in fact had a brother, George, doing just that. Walt had felt the call of the badge, and turned his rather unusual problem solving skills to police work, eventually finding his niche in SWAT. At first, the team had been dubious of his ideas, but as he managed to help out with or even resolve some of their problems, they moved to not only accepting him, but occasionally making suggestions or refinements to his various gadgets. Milan had assembled a modular field kit with all manner of strange devices in it that he could fit together into whatever was needed. For his part in this operation, he had connected a special high quality speaker to a modified remote control helicopter. Walt sent it up the elevator shaft to just under the halted car and, as the other teams began their actions, sent his signal to the speaker, with the sounds of metal clanking, ropes creaking, and men grunting with effort, all in all giving the impression that a team was climbing the shaft beneath the elevator to make some kind of entrance that way. In the unlikely event the sniper could still hear at all after the barrage of flash-bangs, he'd have another source of distraction.

The assault team raced up the final flight of steps, weapons at the ready. The first thing they saw was a shape at one of the windows, bent low over a long rifle, seemingly sighting down the barrel at the street below. Cries of "Drop it" and "Don't move" echoed across the observation deck, but the figure didn't move. Just as they were about to open fire, Roger Brice, the point man, was struck by several shots in the chest. His armor held, but the impact knocked him back and he started to fall, caught at the last moment by Tim Carpenter, next in line on the team. Derick Darby, next up, saw the muzzle flashes coming from the halted elevator, and began filling the space there with short, precision, three round bursts from his AR-15, a "civilian" model of the famed M-16. He was rapidly joined by Brice when he regained his footing and Carpenter once Brice was no longer literally on his hands. They quickly found their mark and Fath let out a grunt of pain and collapsed.

Brice and Carpenter kept their weapons trained on the fallen Fath, and Henderson, fourth in line and leader of the team said into his mic "Target down." then away from it "Smitty, go check the other guy at the window. Matthews, secure the target. You two FNGs" he indicated Farris and Robertson, another officer similarly drafted to make up the numbers of the team "Don't do anything unless I tell you to." Everyone moved to carry out the orders. Smitty, the one with the most medical training, hurried to the side of the man by the window and found he was long dead—the tourist Fath had first shot when taking over the deck, although they didn't know that. His arms had been tied to the rifle, making it look like he was aiming it. Matthews got to the downed terrorist after taking a slightly arcing route instead of moving in a straight line, the better to stay out of the line of fire if the target moved and Brice and Carpenter had to open up again. Matthews saw the man slumped to the floor, bleeding, his right arm extended, and a pistol still gripped in the seemingly lifeless fingers. Just like he'd been trained to, he kicked the weapon away from the man's hand. And set Fath's final surprise in motion.

The weapon skittered across the floor, driven by Matthews' kick. As it moved, it pulled on the fine, nearly invisible fishing line tied to it. The line, in turn, drew out the pins on the two grenades it was tied to. Matthews had time for a startled "Oh, SHIT!" when the explosions rocked the observation deck. Matthews was killed instantly, standing at the center of the blasts. Smitty, kneeling over the beyond help tourist, suffered various wounds from shrapnel and fire, but his body armor took the worst of it. Brice's huge form caught most of the damage rolling toward the stairs and fell, Carpenter dropping beside him. The angle of the stairs and the armor covered bodies of those in front of them protected each person back in line better than the one before. Ironically, Robertson and Fakhoury, pushed to the back because of their "Fucking New Guy" status, were the best protected, even so picking up various cuts as well as a severe ringing in the ears which lasted some time. Structurally, the tower was largely undamaged by the explosions, as the grenades were designed primarily as anti-personnel weapons, not intended to damage harder targets like concrete and steel. There were a few moments of stunned silence, as the very air seemed to echo with the shock of what had just happened, and then screams of pain echoed down the stairs as yet more emergency personnel worked their way upstairs to see to their wounded brethren.

In any conflict, there will be some back and forth, no matter how unevenly matched. To this point, Ammar Hadad's careful planning, overwhelming surprise, and some overall good luck had made things go even better than he had at first hoped. About this time, some good fortune finally came to the other side. Virgil worked for the government, and was high enough up where he was that he generally didn't even tell people which agency he worked for, just dismissed his job as "Oh, I work for the government." This made things easier for him as there was virtually no aspect of his job he was allowed to talk to anyone about. Virgil had first come to government attention when the FCC had arrested him as a young teen. They had gotten complaints about TV interference in one neighborhood, and strange events happening with garage doors. When they finally managed to trace the source of the signals, the agents found his basement workshop, and a device he'd made as a universal remote— but not the usual kind. This one didn't just combine TV and DVR control. He could, with a few adjustments, trigger almost any remote operated device, including all the garage doors. Somewhat embarrassed, he'd explained to the agents that he had just wanted to see if he could do it." A forward thinking senior agent had kept his record clean and arranged a scholarship, with the agreement that Virgil come work for the Federal government when he graduated. Virgil had happily agreed, and had now been working for them for years. Notionally an FCC employee, he had done special work for the FBI, NSA, CIA, and later DHS when it was created. He did no field work, he was no action hero, and knew it. But he could create a staggering array of special technical devices, especially in the fields of radio broadcasting and receiving. One of his most secret projects, and almost never used or even talked about, was a machine that could catch almost any signal—cell phone, radio, wireless Internet, and then run it through various sorting programs he'd created with some help from a few experts. When he'd heard about the sniper, he was horrified like other DC area residents. When he heard about the Mixing Bowl, he grew suspicious, and was already on his way to the special locked room where his "Omni-wave," as he called it, was kept. As the other news rolled in, he turned it on, and placed several buffers to screen out masses of signal traffic. This was too well organized to be some lone extremist like Oklahoma City had been, and it seemed to be still ongoing. He input commands to screen out English language conversations, then figured he'd cycle through the most likely other languages. He'd been getting no useful results until just recently, when moving through Farsi again. There seemed to be a flurry of short messages going back and forth on small hand held radios. He began trying to figure out where they were, when he was confronted with a great example of what some teased him about as his "tunnel vision." A very smart man, and knowing he was smart, he'd been gradually studying various foreign languages, and programming for translations as he went. They'd never be 100% accurate of course, but it was a huge step forward. Unfortunately, he hadn't gotten around to any of the Mid East tongues, partially because of the security issues with his own job. So, now he had some kind of conversation going on, and it sounded tense and stressful to his ear, but he had no idea what they were saying. It had never occurred to him to get help from other people who already knew how to speak the other languages he didn't have. He was sure he could learn them, he just hadn't had time yet.

After a few minutes of frustration, he remembered some of his coworkers talking about a woman at DHS who was trying to build some kind of big talent and information pool. He tried to remember the name, but it wouldn't come, so he ended up calling one of the ones he'd overheard. What followed was an example of why so many odd stories went around about him, especially when he was excited.

Rigby picked up her phone, her eyes still focused on the TV screen and the replayed images of the holocaust at the baseball game. "Yes?" she said absently.

"A few days ago, you were talking to Hines about some woman who was pissing people off by ignoring agency protocol and making her own team from all over. What's her name?"

Rigby blinked and looked at the caller ID screen. "Virgil? What are you talking about?"

He sighed exasperatedly. "Three days ago. Near the coffee machine. Hines was saying this woman was pissing off some director somewhere by not doing things by the book for getting some kind of group together. You said you'd heard she was a good person with good ideas but a 'tough bitch' is what you said. I never heard the name, I was walking past."

"Ohhh. Hanson? What do you need to know about her for?" Rigby was having trouble switching gears and wondering what Virgil was up to now.

"Long story and no time. What's Hanson's number? Or where can I get it?" Virgil was starting to speak faster again, which he did when he was excited or impatient, and now he was both.

"Hold on, I think I have one of her cards or something." She rummaged around in her middle desk drawer, eyes straying back down the hall to the TV someone had brought out to the end of the row of cubicles. Breath mints, rubber bands, paperclips, loose change, a broken cell phone charger, a dried up bottle of correction fluid—when was the last time she'd even bothered to use that?—and then a pile of business cards held together with another rubber band toward the back. She flipped through them, trying to ignore Virgil asking her several times "Do you have it yet?"

Finally she found it and read him the number. As often happened when he had something he'd been asking for, he just hung up with no good bye or thank you. She stared at the phone a moment and shook her head, muttering, "Creepy little techno geek" before going back to watching the news coverage.

Once again, the agents were in Franklin's office. They had simply ignored Mrs. Doorfner and marched past her, pushing the door open, followed by her protests. Franklin looked up at them, a picture of misery. "What do you want?" he asked the trio.

"You didn't just leap to conclusions on that whole Fadad mess. You railroaded the guy, pissed off his brother, and then got someone to clean up after you in the records. He's called you, which you didn't report. So, what else are you not telling us? We're way past covering up for reputation or whatever the hell is going on in your head." Holmes leaned in on Franklin's desk.

Ariel was distracted by her cell phone ringing suddenly. Half surprised she was actually getting a call with all the chaos today, she stepped to the side of the office and answered. "Hanson, DHS."

"You're the one that's getting everyone all ticked off because you're getting people together and sharing information and not playing agency games, right?"

She blinked and looked at the phone's caller ID. It was a government number, but not one she recognized. "I'm sorry, who is this?"

"Right, sorry. My name's Virgil Randolph, I work for the FCC, sorta."

"The FCC? Umm...look, I'm kinda busy today." Ariel began.

"I know, the bombings and all that. I think I have a lead, but I need someone who speaks Farsi. From what I've heard, I figure you might have someone, or know someone who does?"

"What kind of lead?" She covered her ear with her free hand, trying to focus past the argument between Holmes and Franklin. Craigson was looking around the office, studying the walls.

"I have a machine, the Omni-Wave, lets me monitor radio and cell traffic and stuff. I picked up a few things, I think some of them are talking about what happens next, but I don't speak Farsi."

"Your machine can tell you it's Farsi but not translate it?" she asked.

"Yeah, ok, I screwed up. I have it run comparisons on the common words in different languages, but I don't have full translation on all of them. I'm working on it. Anyway, Farsi?" He repeated.

"I don't personally, let me ask a few people. Is this a good number to get back to you on?" She read off the digits on her screen.

"Yeah, if the phones work. I'll be waiting." He hung up.

Ariel shook her head and glanced again at her phone. Strange guy. She looked over and saw Holmes and Franklin glaring at each other. Craigson moved over to her and said quietly, "I think I have an idea about what might be next."

Ariel looked over at the two men locked into staring at each other. Clearly nothing more was going to be gained here. "Ok, Mark, let's go. This isn't getting us anywhere." The silence stretched out for a few moments.

Finally Holmes said "Fine," and followed her out of the office, past the seething Mrs. Doorfner. Ron started to say something, and Holmes bit off "My office." They moved back to Holmes' office in the Counter-Terrorism section.

"OK, what do you two have?" he asked.

Ron and Ariel exchanged glances, and he deferred to her with a hand gesture. "I just got a call from some guy called Randolph, who thinks he's got some radio traffic about today, but while he can identify the language as Farsi, he can't translate it, and says he needs someone who can. You know anyone? Either of you?" She looked at the two FBI Agents.

Ron shook his head and also looked at Mark. The older man was already pulling out his cell phone. "Not off the top of my head, no, but let me try and send out a shout for anyone." He punched in an e-mail to a group of contacts he'd set up on their own list. "Now as long as this signal goes through, we'll see if we can find something. Randolph...isn't he that kinda flaky guy over at FCC?" He asked.

"I don't know him, but he sounded kind of...off." Ariel answered. "What did you have, Ron?"

"I think I have an idea about where else they're going to hit. They seem to be mixing in general terror hits with stuff that's important to Franklin, right?" They both agreed. "I was looking around at his picture wall while Agent Holmes was having that last discussion with him, and I was remembering the stuff I've been hearing about while I've been working with him. He's really big into history in general, and the Smithsonian Museum of American History especially."

"So you think they might try and hit that?" Mark asked.

"Well, seems like a good bet. That or his family." Ron answered.

Holmes nodded. "Anyone know where they are?"

Ron shrugged. "I've left a few messages for the wife and daughter both, but they're not answering."

"Good initiative." Mark complimented him. "When did you do that?"

"While you and Franklin were, um, discussing things." Craigson replied. "Doesn't do us much good if they don't answer, though."

"Fair point. Ariel, can you get plans to the museum while we wait to hear from anyone on this Farsi thing, or Mrs. Franklin, or someone? I'm not sure what else we can do at the moment." The young DHS agent was already pulling out her laptop as he finished his sentence.

Rafe Segovia was tensely staring at the radio rig, waiting for some word. The team had gone in, they had gotten the shooter, it sounded like things were going well, and then there was a deafening sound and there had been nothing for a few minutes. More people were going to check, but no one was rushing into the unknown, so the process was painfully slow. "Come on, come on, how long does it take to get up some damn stairs?" he muttered. Word had gotten around the communication center that one of his trainees had been part of the team, and he was getting a lot of sympathetic looks, which he did his best to ignore. Finally, there was a coughing gasp and "SWAT 5-b to any unit, we need medics up here!"

"5-b, state your condition," Rafe said, feeling some relief, mixed with apprehension for the rest of the team.

"Shooter was rigged, we took him down but then some kind of bomb on him went off a few minutes later. We have multiple officers down up here." Farris coughed again. "And a lot of smoke, but I don't think anything's actually on fire." Farris had been extremely fortunate in his positioning—he'd taken another step or two down the stairs just before the blast, and while he'd been knocked down and stunned, he'd escaped serious injury. The other rookie, Robertson, was still down, possibly with a concussion from what Farris remembered of his first aid training. Upstairs it was much worse. At least two of them were dead, but he was going to let someone else make that official call.

Relief at Farris being relatively unharmed was replaced by concern for the other officers upstairs. Rafe jumped suddenly when his cell vibrated in his pocket. Swatting at it, he pulled it out and saw the text display—"URGENT! Need Farsi speaker re: Today's attacks. Contact ASAP. Holmes, FBI." Rafe looked at it a moment, his mind off in several directions at once. He knew the name Holmes but it wasn't coming to him. Also, despite the fact that it was obvious that's what they were, it was the first time he'd seen today's events called attacks in writing, and for some reason, it shook him up a bit. Then he shook his head a few times to clear it—clearly his priorities were almost as out of whack as his processing ability. He keyed on his mic again "SWAT 5b, roll to," he checked the board for an available channel, "six."

"I'm fine, Rafe," came through as soon as they had both changed.

"That's great kid, really. But this is something else. I got a number for you to call. Well, you might need to text or something, the phones are screwy today. This guy Holmes at the FBI thinks he has a lead on what's going on today, but he needs a Farsi speaker. That's what you speak, right?" Rafe asked.

"Yeah. Ok, give me the number." Rafe read off the digits

and then both returned to the main channel for clean up and status updates on the conditions of the other cops.

Across town, Cynthia Marks parked her car and got out, slamming the door. She'd been in a bad mood all day, made much worse by the explosions and snipers and God only knew what else around the city. She'd been with the others at the office, gathered around the television watching the coverage of everything happening when her supervisor had paged her to his office. They'd been getting complaints from citizens and now government agencies that there was something wrong with the phone system. The number crunchers had torn themselves away from the news long enough to analyze it, and said that the drop in quality was too big for just the flood of anxious phone calls as friends and family tried to check on each other amid all the chaos. They'd tried to get a status report from the major phone node, but no one was answering land lines, cells, texts, or e-mails, when the various calls went through. So, someone had to go over and provide a report—"someone" spelled C I N D Y, apparently. Like she didn't have enough to do. She got up to the door and pressed the intercom button. A few minutes passed and there was no answer. She pressed again several times, with similar results, or lack thereof. Having tried to do things the "polite" way, she fished out the set of keys she'd been issued to gain entry if there was some kind of problem. She worked through the ring, and finally got to the right key on her fifth try. Nothing could be simple today, could it? she thought to herself. She turned the key, pulled the door open, and triggered Nazzir's parting gift. The explosion blew her back across the walk to land on the hood of her own car, the heavy door landing on top of her a half second later. Fire rushed out of the entrance, and back down the hallway. The overworked emergency services units in the city would have another call to respond to, but it was too late for Cindy, and there would be no quick fix for the phones, that was certain.

As Farris tried unsuccessfully to call Agent Holmes, Wanda finally got her own call to go through. As soon as she heard the phone being picked up, she got out a half sobbing "Bernie?"

He let out a sigh of relief. "Wanda? Is that you? Are you ok?"

"They killed Gina, Bernie. And all those people at the game, and on the bridge…I sent in a report, but I don't know what I'm supposed to do now." she was feeling weak with relief at getting hold of him, of anyone the way things were going today, and her self control, that she'd been clutching at with her fingertips, was finally cracking.

"Gina? Damn it, how'd that happen? Never mind….you're ok, though? Where are you, anyway?" he asked.

"Yes, I'm fine, I was up in the helicopter, they almost hit us going in but Mike did some fantastic flying, and then Hector knocked one of them out with a pitch and he fell, and then they crashed, and." she tried to pull herself together.

"I know, Wanda, I saw it. I got the feed from you and Gina both. You both did great work. But now you've got to get back here." Bernie told her.

"Back there? How? Why? What's going on?" she asked.

"If you're in the chopper, you can get back here easier than about anyone else, and that's part of the problem. Diane is stuck out in the traffic somewhere," I hope, he added silently to himself, "and everyone else is busy on different aspects or trapped at home. You've seen this, you've got a first hand account, we need you back here and on the air." Bernie paused. "Can you do it?"

Any other day, the answer would have been an unhesitating "Of course I can." Today, Wanda had seen a new friend killed, hundreds of others injured or killed, and the disasters had kept coming in as the day progressed. She bit her lip for a moment then said, "Yeah, I'll get there.

Gonna need a hell of a makeup job though."

He let out a small laugh. "I'll get Ray on stand by. Get yourself here, Wanda. And I'm glad you're all right."

Wanda turned to tell Mike their new destination, then noticed they were almost there. "How'd you know?" she asked.

"You've been kinda out of it, understandably. I did a few sweeps over the city to get more footage, got ordered to put down by a really pissed off Air Traffic Control guy, and headed for the studio about when you finally got through." Mike answered.

As Mike brought them down on to the helipad, Ariel was working her computer, a faint feeling of something else being wrong creeping along the edges of her brain. Holmes and Craigson were debating what to try and do about the Smithsonian, and the perceived threat there, but Ariel wasn't really listening as she followed a hunch. She used her own skills and some priority codes she'd been given a while ago to begin accessing some files of Fowler's. The dead agent may have had questionable taste in lovers, but her investigative skills had been formidable. Something wasn't seeming right to her. The information about Hadad she'd been able to find suggested he was a cold, calculating, ruthless planner. Diverting resources from a major strike just to torment Franklin seemed out of character to her, even with his brother taken into account. Ariel kept rooting around in restricted directories that Fowler was keeping, and was beginning to find some things she wasn't liking at all. She kept looking, frowning and making notes, fleshing out her theory. Holmes broke off when his phone buzzed, and he read a text, then punched in a response. "Who was that?" Craigson asked.

"Cop one of my guys knows from that alert I sent out on what Ariel got. Says he speaks Farsi, I told him to get with Randolph." Holmes answered.

"You think this Randolph guy really has something?" Craigson asked. Ariel was paying a bit more attention at the moment, her attention captured when she heard her name and glanced around to make sure she hadn't missed something.

"If he says he does, I believe it. I've heard about this guy, he's supposed to be amazing with radio and communication stuff. He's forgotten more about that kind of thing than the three of us will ever know." Holmes said.

"Why is that supposed to be comforting or mean something?" Ariel asked. The others turned to look at her. "I mean, if he forgot it, and we don't know it, then we can't get to the information anyway, so why does it help anything or why is it supposed to be impressive?"

As Craigson and Holmes looked blankly at each other, trying to come up with an explanation for a phrase that really didn't make much sense, events continued to wrack the city. People who hear about Washington, DC, end up hearing about the Potomac River. It runs to the west of the city, between the Lincoln Memorial on the DC side and Arlington Cemetery across on the Virginia shore. There is also the persistent folk tale of a young George Washington throwing a silver dollar across the river. Anyone who looks at the actual river realizes that this is some classic tall tale telling, or Mr. Washington was born some two hundred years too early and would have been the greatest pitcher baseball has ever seen.

Much less is heard of the Anacostia River. It forms the city's eastern boundary, and flows along beside no great memorials or monuments, but rather some of the poorer areas of the Capitol, likely contributing to its obscurity. The major crossing of the Anacostia is the Frederick Douglas Bridge, named after the escaped slave who later learned to write and read and became a skilled speaker. The history of this name, however, was lost on the man who called himself Shakir. His taking a special *nom de guerre* may have been a tribute to Nazzir, who had become something of a legend among some terrorists, or may have been more towards keeping his own origins secret and sparing his family the repercussions of his actions.

While many of those who were working in one way or another under Hadad's direction in the attacks on the Capitol today were young impressionable men, the stereotype of the recruited martyr, Shakir was quite a bit older. He had fought in Afghanistan against the Russian invasion. It was there he had picked up a special skill. One of the ways the Americans had subtly, or not so subtly, aided the Muslims against the Communists was supplying a very large number of shoulder fired Stinger missiles. When the war was over and the Russians retreated in defeat, large numbers of those missiles were unaccounted for. Shakir had been noted for his skill with the weapons, and had now brought some of the missing devices back to America, albeit not in a way they were likely to appreciate.

While the destruction wrought at various other highways would leave lasting marks and take considerable time and effort to repair, it wasn't the only way to proceed about the day's business. The Stinger was designed to be an anti-aircraft weapon, but just about any kind of weapon can be modified by a skilled hand. Shakir was on top of a stopped van, in turn atop one of the highway overpasses that overlooked the Douglas Bridge. He had a few men detailed to guard him in case the police were more vigilant than was believed likely, or someone else decided to become involved. Shakir had heard the increasingly frantic news reports that indicated his brethren were doing well with their appointed tasks, and that it was now his turn. He sighted in on a large semi trailer (sadly, no convenient fuel truck presented itself and they had not arranged for one here as they had at the Mixing Bowl), and fired off his first missile, not bothering to watch as it streaked off and he reached for another tube. The missile flew low over the roadway, startling the few motorists not too wrapped up in trying to figure out why their cell phone calls weren't going through to notice it, and then impacted the large truck. The explosion destroyed the cab, turning it into an inferno and sending bits of shrapnel everywhere. As stunned motorists were trying to take in what had happened, Shakir fired again, immolating an SUV near the already burning truck. Panic began to spread at the second explosion, and drivers began frantically trying to speed away, reverse along the bridge, or come to a complete stop as seemed best to each. Many more accidents occurred in the spreading reaction, and Shakir destroyed another vehicle, this time a pick up truck, before switching to the other side of the bridge and starting to take out some of the inbound traffic as well. Soon, the bridge was a mess of blazing cars, multiple accidents, screaming civilians, and people suffering various degrees of injury. No one would be leaving, or entering, the city by this route any time soon. One aggressive would-be hero had tried to interfere with Shakir, and his assigned body guards had blasted him with a hail of AK-47 fire, then sprayed down another passing car in a fit of exuberance. Shakir shook his head at the needless waste of ammunition, but then, he thought, boys will be boys.

Farris made his way through the city, not even changing out of his borrowed SWAT gear. The police radio was flooded with calls, back up needed at the sites devastated earlier, still new attacks being reported, and a few "regular" criminals taking advantage of the chaos to try their various robberies, burglaries, or whatever their crime of choice was. Farris felt guilty about not helping, but Agent Holmes had been very insistent that Farris needed to get to the address he'd been given and assist someone who needed his translation skills. Having gotten almost used to the concept of the cell phones largely not working, he was startled when his rang suddenly. Veering around traffic slow downs and tie ups, and ignoring the DC traffic law about not using cell phones while driving, he answered his, hoping for some more useful information about what was happening.

He was surprised once again when he heard a familiar voice in Farsi in his ear. "What is happening in your crazy city? Are you all right? Are you safe?"

He waited for a break in the flow of words. "Mother, please, I'm fine. I'm doing my duty and trying to stop this madness." He dodged what appeared to be an abandoned Metro bus in the right lane, halfway up on the curb.

She sighed, "Of course you are. I would expect no less of you, although sometimes I believe you take your name too seriously." Farris meant Knight in old Arabic, and he'd been teased about it often enough while growing up, both within and outside the family.

"That's me, off to save the world on my trusty camel." he joked. "Speaking of, I need to go now, Mother, I have to meet someone. I love you, and tell father that, too."

"I love you too, Farris. Take care of yourself, you don't need to be the only hero in the city. And besides, Mrs. Farreell down the block just had her niece move in with her, from Oman. She's a lovely girl."

Farris grimaced at the phone and hung up. He stopped the car and regarded the building, double checking the address. This looked more like a small business than a government office, but it matched the number Holmes had texted him. Farris looked around again and mounted the steps, seeing the intercom button and pressing it.

Waiting a few minutes, he heard a tinny sounded voice "Yes?"

"I was given this address by Mark Holmes, he said someone here needed a translator." Farris spoke into the grille, noticing the camera mounted above the door.

"And you speak Afghani?" the voice asked.

Farris frowned. "I was told you needed Farsi, I don't have

any Afghani."

"Just testing." The door buzzed and opened. "Come in, down the hall, and take the elevator down to the bottom."

Farris pushed the door open and walked forward down a very threadbare looking corridor to an elevator. As he pressed the call button, he heard the door close behind him. His first thought was "This guy's seen too many movies." He took the elevator down and when the doors opened, saw a huge array of all manner of technological bits and pieces. "Looks like Frankenstein's lab," he muttered to himself.

"I'd prefer Edison's, or Tesla's." The voice was recognizable from the speaker as a thin man moved out from behind some large device whose purpose Farris couldn't even guess at. "Virgil Randolph. I need you over here."

He led the officer down a narrow path among the gadgets. Farris followed, bemused, and when they reached a large machine that looked like it was connected to several powerful computers. "I'm Officer Farris Fakhoury," he tried to begin.

Randolph waved his hand back and forth. "Yeah, ok. Look, here's how it works. You've heard that thing in the movies about 'if I told you, I'd have to kill you'?"

Farris nodded, thinking, "I knew this guy was a movie nut."

"Ok, the real version is more like if you start talking about the stuff I have to show you, I end up making calls and you, and whoever you told, and whoever they talked to, disappear." Farris half expected a laugh, but none came. "So, keep it a secret, and it's all good. I can monitor a lot of stuff with this, I call it an Omni-Wave. Is that too comic booky?" he asked suddenly.

Farris looked back at him. "Umm....maybe a little."

"Ok, better name later I guess. Anyway, this can pick up all kinds of stuff, but I don't use it much so all the lawyers don't start lecturing at me and my boss. Anyway, I fired it up when all this crap started going on today, and this is some of what I got. You ready?" Farris looked at the odd blonde man and nodded.

Randolph flipped a switch and a high quality recording of a conversation, evidently over hand held radios, began playing. Farris concentrated and grabbed the nearby pad and pen, writing as they went. This would take a while, he thought as he settled into a nearby chair.

Back across town, Agent Craigson excused himself, saying he wanted to take care of something in person since the phones were currently unreliable at best. After he left, Holmes continued paging through some of the notes they'd come up with and said without looking up, "So, what's bothering you, Ariel?"

She was a bit startled. "Have I told you it's creepy when you do that?" she asked.

"Yes. Now quit stalling. You bumped into something that's giving you some trouble somewhere along the way here. What is it? You're vibrating like you've had even more coffee than me." He looked across at her and waited.

"Ok, well, I'm not one hundred percent on this yet," she began.

"Reservations and disclaimers noted. Go on," he answered.

"Well, everything I can find on this Hadad guy, if that's who this is, says he's a cold, smooth operator. A real hard case. So I was thinking, this is someone who gets all bent out of shape about his brother? I was wondering about what else might be going on. From the little bit we got out of Franklin, and a bit more from a few other places, it sounded like Hadad had a lot on him really quickly. Which made me think he had help." Hanson paused again, looking over at Holmes.

"Someone was giving him information?" he asked.

"I think so. Then I began wondering who, and who'd have a lot on Franklin," she continued.

"You think Fowler was supplying him?" Holmes asked her.

"No, actually I don't. I think she was on to who was."

Holmes looked at her. "Then who—Conroy? You think it was Conroy? The guy's a legend, he's one of the last real old school agents."

"Yes, old school, and a bit old himself, and facing a retirement that was forced on him by the age limit. Our retirement package isn't bad, but it's not as good as active duty. And numbers is what Fowler was good at, remember?"

"She was investigating him?" Holmes asked, a bit unbelievingly.

"I think so. I haven't had a chance to go all through her files yet. Think about it, she's spending all this time with Franklin, and then hears something wrong about Conroy—everyone says he and Franklin were really tight. But then something or other changed, maybe the economic meltdown, and Conroy asked for more or something? That or the timing of them coming now was just coincidence. But think about it—everything they've done today has been a decent target for a terrorist, except Conroy and Fowler. What if it's not about screwing with Franklin? What if that part is getting rid of a loose end, and the woman who was closing in on him?" Hanson looked back at him. "I need more time, so it will have to wait, but from what I've got so far, I think that's what happened."

Holmes thought about that. "It makes sense, but it's not definite one way or the other. And then what were the phone calls about?"

"Family is supposed to be very important in Arabic culture. It might not be to him, but it's supposed to be. So if he makes it look like he orchestrated all this just for his brother, he becomes a legend, a folk hero almost, right?"

Holmes nodded slowly. "Yeah, he might. That's some good thinking. Does that mean he's not going after the

Museum, like Craigson thought?"

Hanson shrugged. "I don't see why not, it's a decent target for them. But I can't swear to it either way. He probably wouldn't mind some payback on Franklin, but if I'm right, it's not his major focus."

Back at Randolph's lab, Farris held up his hand. "Wait, play that again."

Randolph pressed the right buttons, and Farris nodded. "Ok, got it. Most of this is just vague communication, they're being good about not giving things away on the radio. But that last part, one of them gets all emotional, proud of himself. He's saying they are going to destroy the collection of false idols that Americans worship, and they will cover America's glory with their own." Randolph looked blankly at him. "I'm betting that means it's the American History Museum. You know, Old Glory, the big flag? It's in the main lobby there." Farris tried his cell, and as he expected, he couldn't get through. He looked at the so-called "Omni-Wave." and thought about it a moment. "Can this thing send out, too?"

Randolph nodded "Yeah, but it's only good for a short message. It has some side effects I haven't balanced out yet."

"Ok, let me know when you can do it, I don't have that much I need to tell them." Farris knew what he wanted to say, and was ready. He waited impatiently for Randolph to finish making adjustments. Randolph nodded finally, and Farris punched in the number. A somewhat surprised sounding Agent Holmes picked up a few moments later, his own name sounding more a question than a statement "Holmes?"

"Agent Holmes, it's Officer Farris. They're going after the Smithsonian Museum of American History, specifically Old Glory it sounds like. Not sure how long I have, Randolph jury rigged something here."

"Ok. We're going to try and get some people in place

over there if we can. Everyone's really spread out by now, which may have been part of the plan in the first place. Thank you for your help, and I don't think I need to say this is classified material." Holmes added the last as an afterthought.

"I got that lecture or warning or whatever it is already, thanks." The connection broke off, and several cell phones in the immediate area had their receivers destroyed by the power of the carrier wave Randolph had used to cut through the over burdened signal traffic.

Farris put down his phone and picked up the rest of his gear he'd removed to get more comfortable. Randolph looked over at him "Where are you going?"

"If they're going to attack the Museum, and everyone's so thin personnel wise already, they're going to need help. So I'm going there."

Randolph shook his head. "That's crazy. You're going to get yourself killed."

Farris moved to the elevator. "Well, first off, it's part of my job to protect the city, and secondly, if I do get killed, I won't give away your secrets down here, will I?"

Randolph looked after him and went back to his desk and computer, idea for refining a new design flickering around in his head. People like Farris could have the shoot outs, he'd be happy to stay down here and keep working. He checked to make sure the officer left, and then clicked all the locks and reset the alarms so he wouldn't be disturbed.

As Holmes shared this confirmation with Ariel, Wanda sat behind the anchor desk, trying to get herself under control. Ray had done his usual amazing job, and she looked a lot less ragged than when she had arrived back at the studio. His deft touch left her looking serious, and not at all glamorous, befitting the news of the day. She adjusted her papers in front of her, unwilling to take a chance on just the teleprompter today.

Bernie stood beyond the cameras, looking at Wanda. He'd just tried to reach Diane again, with no luck. He hoped it was just the telephone problem everyone seemed to be having, and that she wasn't another casualty of today's insanity. In the meanwhile, with people missing, trapped behind the carnage on the roads, or already on assignment elsewhere, Wanda was the best he had. Also, she had seen some of this first hand, and would likely have some more unique commentary. He hoped she was up to it, but he was fairly certain she was.

Wanda watched Pete, the floor director. He counted down on his fingers and then pointed at the camera directly in front of her. She looked into it and began. "This is a Newsline Special Report. As you are probably aware, Washington, DC, has suffered a series of attacks this afternoon. They seem to be the work of a dedicated, organized group. Hundreds of lives have been lost so far, and millions of dollars worth of property damage has been done in and around the city. We will keep you updated as more information becomes available to us. At the moment, let's turn to Roger Travis, who is at the site of one of the most devastating of these attacks, the Mixing Bowl in Fairfax County. Roger?"

When the camera cut away to an on the scene report, she breathed a sigh of relief and rolled her shoulders. Bernie walked over to her. "You ok?"

"Yeah, I'm fine. I think. It's just been a really rough day already, and this is my first time at this desk. I'll be ok." She resolutely pushed aside thoughts of everything she'd seen at Nationals Park.

"I know you will. Just take a deep breath and go with the story. You'll do great." Bernie smiled at her and moved back away from camera range. Wanda watched the remote reporter discussing what little was known so far about the destruction of the highway overpass. The camera crew had arrived and set up just in time to see another major section of the weakened "fly ramp" as the tall structures were called, collapse on to the roadway below, now blocking off the south bound lanes as the northern ones had been by the initial explosion. There was another sudden stir of activity in the studio, and Wanda looked at the teleprompter, at the same time hearing directions in her ear piece.

"Roger, I'm sorry to interrupt, but we've just had another development. We don't have video yet, but we have confirmed reports that the Tuckerman Lane overpass on Route 270 North has been destroyed. 270 is now also no longer reachable from the Beltway. Experts are refusing to comment, but it does seem a recurring theme of these assaults on our area that transportation routes are being targeted." Wanda listened for a moment. "We're going to take you now to the Old Post Office Pavilion, where the sniper who terrorized the area was slain just a short time ago. Renee, what can you tell us?"

Ammar Hadad smiled to himself as he watched the news. Yes, highways and the like had been a part of his plan. He also quite deliberately left untouched one major route out of Washington, DC. Ammar had studied his craft well, and read teaching of various great strategists. Sun Tzu had said something to the effect of "If you leave the enemy no escape, they will fight ten times harder. Leave them a path to flee, and they will." So Ammar had not done anything to Route 66 out of the west end of the city. He reckoned, and correctly from other reports he was receiving, that the various law enforcement agencies would waste resources safe guarding a place he had no interest in, and that the panicking citizens fleeing would add to the chaos and destruction on their own. From the number of accidents being reported, that was coming to pass. He checked his watch. Quite soon now it would be time to move along to the next phase of his plan.

Holmes looked across the desk at Ariel, putting his phone

down. "I can't reach most of the people on my list, and the ones I can get can't help. They planned this really well. Everyone's all tied up with bridge collapses, bombings, and that sniper, along with whatever else they dreamed up we don't even know about yet."

"So what are we going to do?" she asked him, still working a few things on her computer.

"Well, if it is the Smithsonian they're going after, we might be it. So I guess we'll need to gear up and get over there."

Ariel stopped typing and looked at him closely. "Us. The investigator, the computer geek, and the rookie?"

"Wouldn't be my first pick, but seems like that's what we have. You have a better idea that doesn't involve letting them blow up priceless national treasures?" Holmes raised his eyebrows. "If you do, I'm all ears."

She sighed. "No, not really. I guess it's time to do this."

"I guess that's my cue." They both turned as Craigson came in carrying various bags, some in his hands, some slung over his shoulders.

"What's all that?" Ariel asked, eyeing the bundles.

"Armor, weapons, extra ammunition, radios, lights, night vision gear." They both stared at him. "I have a friend in HRT, I know where they keep the spare gear."

Holmes regarded him silently a moment. "You raided a Hostage Rescue Team supply cache?"

"Right now, they don't need it. We do. Plus, we don't actually have an HRT here, this is extra gear that's been repaired or newly ordered but not shipped yet." Craigson began opening bags and cases and laying out equipment. "Anything you have questions on, ask." The other two watched him quickly organize an impressive arsenal of weapons and support equipment and then began preparing themselves.

Traffic was snarling up all over the Washington, DC, area.

Almost every major route into the city had been damaged, destroyed, or attacked in some way. The ones that had not were choked with people fleeing the Capitol, slowed even more by the inevitable string of accidents as distracted and terrified drivers were forced together in heavier and heavier traffic. DC is a city of multiple jurisdictions, with local police and numerous federal agencies throughout the city. But between the number of attacks, the poisoning of large numbers of the Metropolitan Police Department, and the inability for those outside the city to easily get back in, response times were long and getting longer. And of course, with the phones not working correctly, reporting new problems or coordinating mutual aid added even more time.

Wanda watched the stories about the sniper, and the lives he'd taken, civilian and police both, ending with the horrific explosion on top of the tower. There was a piece covering what they knew of the bombs apparently going off in the Metro's Yellow Line Tunnel. Then it was back to her.

"I was present for the attack at Nationals Park. A group of terrorists in a helicopter strafed the crowd, people who had come to see the game, and to help with the charity match between the teams from the Senate and the House. I saw Hector Valdez stand up to them, and actually bring down a terrorist with his legendary fastball." Her voice over was being heard as the footage from the Park was being shown. "I saw a valiant police officer try and halt the slaughter. And then they crashed into the field, creating a firestorm that claimed an as yet unknown number of lives, including Hector Valdez and Gina Wright, a camerawoman for this station, and my friend." Her voice almost broke but she managed to continue. "We will be bringing you more information as we get it. For now, we urge everyone to stay at home, stay safe, and if you see something suspicious, try hard to report it. We have several emergency numbers being shown on the screen now, for the police, the FBI, and the Department of

Homeland Security. We know the telephones aren't working very well today, and we're told people are looking into that, too. But be patient, and keep trying if you've seen something. Our coverage will continue in just a moment." The lights on the cameras went dark as they cut to special messages from the people they'd been able to get hold of in the government so far. Wanda went over her papers and prepared for the next segment.

In his basement lab, Virgil Randolph kept working. The intercepts seemed like they'd been useful, but he wasn't done. He was carefully eliminating all the signals he could account for, and all the private ones he could find out anything about. Using the various programs he'd helped write or hired out, and the scanning equipment he'd designed and built, he planned on managing to isolate the signals and trace their locations. Then he'd let one of the agent type people go deal with them and go back to more interesting work.

Nabil al-Nadir was growing impatient. He'd been listening to the radio and heard the reports of his brothers-in-arms successes today. But he was holding his team of men back, awaiting the signal. He had spoken some with Haroun, who they had stationed as a lookout, but their area was clear. There was no sign anyone knew they were here. So, they waited. And waited. The day seemed as though it would never end, that their time would never come. But finally, Ferran shouted from the computer he'd been assigned to watch. "We have our message!" Nabil hurried over and looked at the screen. GO FORTH AND DESTROY THEIR IDOLS. GOD IS MOST GREAT. Nabil gave a shout of triumph.

"To the trucks, everyone! Get your weapons and prepare to strike the un-Godly!" he commanded. There was a rush of running feet, the click of magazines being checked a final time, and doors slamming. At last, they could show that they, too, were warriors. Remembering the instructions for their departure, he ran across to the table they had all been instructed to not even approach until this moment. He raised a small plastic shield, pressed the switch it was covering, and ran for the truck, yelling "Now, now, we must go now!" As the bay door raised on the rented garage that had done no auto repair in quite some time, the three trucks roared out. As they got to the corner and turned left, towards the National Mall, the building they had exited suddenly detonated, igniting yet another fire in the over burdened city. Their orders had been clear—destroy it on the way out or if the police or government came snooping around. This would cause more chaos and remove any trace evidence they had left, further confounding their efforts later to determine who was behind this and where they had come from. They would know what the leader chose to tell them, and nothing more.

Signing out a large SUV from the motor pool, Craigson drove while Holmes tried to see if he could raise anymore help on his various cell phones and Blackberry and Ariel sent out urgent messages on her laptop. None of them were sure if any help was coming, or if they would be the only ones there. They also had no idea of what the enemy force would be like. Scarcely the ideal way to go into a fight, but they hadn't had a lot of choices. Hopefully luck would turn their way, which wasn't much to pin a combat plan on, but it was all they had. Trying to ease the tension, Craigson turned on the radio. The lyrics to an Eric Clapton song filled the vehicle "Ma, take these guns away from me…'cuz I can't shoot them anymore…it's getting dark, too dark to see…feels like I'm knockin' on Heaven's door." Hurriedly he turned it back off and smiled embarrassedly. "I hope that wasn't an omen," he thought. The others thought much the same, but no one spoke the thought aloud. As it turned out, it was, for at least one of them.

Farris Fakhoury picked up his radio mic and paused for a moment. He wasn't sure which way to identify himself at first, but decided to revert to his badge number. "7412 to dispatch."

"7412, wait one." There was a pause. "Roll to three."

He switched over and heard "You ok, kid? You dropped off the grid for a while." Rafe's voice came over the speaker.

"Yeah, I had to go see," he thought about how to phrase it, "some of those people you sent me to."

"Ok. What's going on?" the older man's voice sounded worried.

"I'm not sure what I'm allowed to say about most of it, but if you can find anyone not already on assignment, I think we need as many as we can at the Museum of American History." Farris was doing his best to weave around the admittedly lighter than normal traffic as he talked.

Rafe put the mic down to his chest while he surveyed the screen detailing who was doing what where. "I don't think we have anyone, we're down too many as it is. Bunch too sick to work, a lot more can't get anywhere, and we lost a lot at the Park, and a few more at the Douglas Bridge."

What the hell happened at the Douglas? Farris wondered, but decided he'd only deal with one thing at a time. "Ok then, mark me en route to the Museum, and if you get me anyone, send back up. It's sounding like it's going to be ugly."

"You take care of yourself. Rafe's rule number 3 is?" he asked.

"Heroes look good on TV but you don't want to be one or work with one." Farris dutifully recited. "But sometimes there really isn't a choice, Rafe. Rolling back to one."

Rafe stared at his mic and wondered if this day was ever going to end.

Gerry Franklin regarded his telephone suspiciously as it rang. He felt like his spirits couldn't get any lower, and yet dreaded any more news. Finally he picked it up. "Franklin."

"Gerry, I wasn't sure I'd get through with all the difficulty the phones are having. I suppose that's what happens when you stir up all manner of trouble and then destroy a lot of the support equipment for the phone system." The voice was taunting him again.

"What do you want Hadad?" He asked wearily.

"I have most of what I want already. Shame about your wife and daughter being on the bridge at just the wrong time. It's almost like it was planned."

"Is there a point to this, or are you just gloating now, you sonovabitch?" Franklin's voice rasped.

"Gerry, I've asked you to mind your language and try and stay professional. I just wanted to say that I'm sorry it looks like we're going to miss each other this time. Perhaps I can catch you on my next trip to your lovely city. Well, after some repairs anyway." The mocking voice was finally getting some reaction from him. "I only have one more stop to make before I leave."

"What stop? Where are you going?" he snapped.

"Well, I know it's captivated your attention over the years, one of the few things to really hold your interest long term, actually. So I thought I should see what this Museum of American History of yours is like. Good bye, Gerry." The phone suddenly went dead in his ear. Franklin glared at it and felt rage building within him. He yanked the phone off the desk suddenly and threw it across the room. Mrs. Doorfner appeared in the doorway, concern on her face, and he waved her off. One look at his expression and she retreated.

The small convoy of trucks turned down Madison Avenue on the National Mall and screeched to a halt in front of the American History Museum. In a stroke of misfortune, one of the few Park Police left in the area saw them and came running over. "Hey, buddy, you can't park here," he began. The first man out of the truck turned and simply shot him. The rest of the men climbed out and got their weapons ready.

Farris pulled his cruiser back in a hurry. He'd seen them gun the officer down, and he knew he was too late. He called in a hurried radio update requesting back up and medics, but didn't stay to hear the response. He got out, easing the door shut behind him, and nervously gripped his weapon. He still had the rifle he'd been issued by the SWAT unit, what felt like a lifetime ago. He moved up to the side of the Museum, glancing backward at the Natural History Museum next door. In the wake of the attacks, the buildings had been closed early, and the usually omnipresent tourists seemed to have vanished. That was at least one less thing to worry about.

He crouched at the corner, making himself as small a target as possible and began aiming his rifle.

Craigson drove faster, but better, than the other two agents would have given him credit for. It seemed the rookie had some surprising skills. They whipped around the corner and saw Constitution Avenue was mostly clear, a rare sight in daylight hours. Making the next turn fast enough to send Ariel grabbing for the handle to hold, they sped up towards the front of the museum and saw several men walking away from some trucks and what looked like a body on the ground.

Nabil walked toward the Museum entrance, not sparing a glance for the man that Rakin had shot down. He saw the doors were closed, and presumably locked, and a security guard inside was looking out at him quizzically, not being able to make out what had just happened. He was about to give the first command to deal with the doors when a large SUV rushed around the corner and squealed to a halt. The doors opened and several heavily armed people got out and began crouching behind the vehicle, using it for cover. Clearly, there would be some actual fighting, enough to get a man's blood flowing. That was fine with Nabil. He turned towards them and began firing, his rounds raking the side of the car, joined a moment later by his comrades as they punched hole after hole in the side panels.

"SHIT!" Ariel cursed, ducking behind the engine block. This was a lot of fire, and there were more men than they'd hoped. Ron dropped to the ground beside her and she thought at first that he'd been hit, but then she saw him lying down and lining up on the feet and lower legs of the enemy. He fired a three round burst, dropping one of them with a yelp of pain. Holmes rolled around the end of the SUV and fired a quick burst as well, ducking back behind it when answering fire almost obliterated the corner of their car. "Boy, motor pool is gonna hate us," Ariel caught herself thinking as she flinched when another round took off a piece of the hood near her head.

Nabil gestured for his men to spread out, furious that one had been wounded before they even got into the museum. They began moving apart so they couldn't be hit by the same spray of fire. How many were back there, Nabil wondered. Two? Three maybe? This shouldn't be too much more than a temporary distraction.

Farris had waited when the firing started, wanting to see what happened and make sure he knew who he should be aiming at. He'd guess the edge of the car he could just barely see had carried some of the good guys, and the ones coming from the rental trucks were the bad guys. Seeing the weapons out and in use, and the murder of the Park Police officer, he figured the standard police warning was no longer needed. Reacquiring his target from before, he let out a slow breath and gently squeezed the trigger.

Nabil was stunned when it suddenly seemed that Dabir's head simply exploded next to him. He realized they were under fire from another attacker in a different direction. Turning, he fired at the corner of the building, spraying fire ineffectively in his first hurried reaction. He barked out an order, and two more of his men redirected their fire as well, turning away from the SUV.

Ron rolled away from where he'd been lying as one of the terrorists began spraying fire low, skipping the rounds up off the courtyard's surface. Ariel edged around the front and let off a burst of her own, hitting one of them more by luck than skill. She'd be among the first to admit that while her computer skills were second to few, if any, she was not equally adept with a gun, and sometimes barely squeaked through the annual certification for firearms. She jumped back under cover as more shots concentrated on her side again. Ron yelled out to Holmes "Looks like we have a friend over there. Any idea who it is?"

Holmes shook his head. "Does it matter? Long as he's shooting them and not us." He risked another shot over the roof of the now very chewed up vehicle and ducked low again.

Nabil was getting over stunned and working on enraged. His men were exposed out here in the courtyard approach to the entrance, and taking fire from two sides. He glanced back at the trucks and remembered that being near them in a firefight was probably an even worse option. He commanded his men to keep up their fire and then ran forward at the entrance, leveling his weapon and firing off a blast on full automatic. The glass entryway was tough, but was never designed to stand up to such a concentrated attack, and gave way as the magazine ran out. Nabil reloaded, looking ahead cautiously for the security personnel he presumed were there somewhere. Not seeing any, he kicked the broken glass aside and moved in to the vestibule, turning to the right to get around the glass wall and looking past the unmanned metal detectors at the entry.

Farris saw the man running forward and tried to hit him, but he was soon past the somewhat limited angle he had from the corner. Cursing, he shifted his fire back to main group and dropped another terrorist. He heard a tell tale click and ejected the spent magazine, reaching for a new one, and hoping more help was on the way. He fired another short burst and then ducked back as bullets knocked up stone chips all around him.

Holmes and Craigson both called out "Got one!" at the

same time. The terrorists were dropping fast, being pinned between two attacks with virtually no cover. The only reason they weren't going down faster was the heavy return fire. Another one sprinted ahead and no one managed to pick him off as he made it to the doors. Craigson cursed and focused again on the ones remaining. They needed to put these guys down before too many more made it inside.

On the Constitution Avenue side of the building, the cleaning staff were fleeing the building. They weren't entirely sure what was happening around front, but it sounded like World War III was going on, and they had no interest in dying in the name of cleaning the building. Several of the security staff, who were unarmed, tried to keep the mass exodus as orderly as they could. With the understandable desire to get away from the heavy automatic weapons fire, no one really worried about the one figure moving against the flow, working its way inside the building.

Farid dropped to one knee to make himself a smaller target. The heavy resistance had surprised them all, and he could see this was going badly for them. Several of them had been killed already. He was willing to die in the name of his cause, but he would not go alone. He found a surprising calm within himself and steadied his weapon.

Ariel popped up over the hood again and fired a few more shots. Cursing, she saw she'd missed and she tried to get a good line on another one. Suddenly, she was on the ground, her breath labored. What just happened? Where was her gun? She had to get back up, the others needed her. But maybe in just minute, a short rest first. Funny, she hadn't realized it had gotten so close to sunset already, but it was getting dark so quickly now...

"Ariel!" Mark shouted, seeing her fall. Ron immediately changed his aim and shot the man who had dropped her. "Ariel, are you ok? C'mon, say something!" Mark kept looking back at her and firing back at them alternately. Mark

Holmes had a reputation for being a cold hearted man, but he was in a rage now. He and Ron, without exchanging a word, began working on the outer edges of the group of remaining targets and working their way in. Several more fell to their renewed fire.

Franklin stopped his car by the Museum's Constitution Avenue entrance. He heard gunfire being exchanged, and got out of the car. He'd taken enough today, been pushed too far. His career was probably over, his family was dead, his dead beat brother finally in jail for something he couldn't smooth over, Jill was gone, and for all he knew he was still under suspicion for that. This place had inspired him, interested him, and housed treasures. He remembered Ronnie abandoning her teenager's carefully practiced cool when he'd shown her the room with Kermit in it. Ronnie…he shook his head. She was gone now, too. He crept along the edge of the building, his service weapon out. He saw a man in riot gear crouched at the corner, firing some kind of assault rifle at unseen enemies. Franklin hastily backtracked and moved around to the other side, running and then walking, feeling all the time he'd put in at his desk, all the times he'd resolved to work out more and then not done it. He came up the other side, and saw tire tracks across the stone courtyard. More fire was coming from this side, it sounded like. He carefully moved forward, trying to avoid accidentally becoming a friendly fire statistic. He peered around the corner and saw a shot-to-bits SUV with two men behind it firing at a group out in the center area. One of them looked like Craigson, he thought. There was a slightly smaller figure lying on the ground behind them, a crimson stain spreading out around it. He took one more step, trying to find an angle where he could help the Agents (he presumed the man with Craigson was an agent) without startling them into shooting him. He thought about shouting, but thought that could be just as bad, and might distract one at a critical time. He moved a bit further forward, still undecided about what he should do. He never heard the shot—he couldn't have anyway; the weapon was silenced. Franklin fell to the ground, a new third eye of blood suddenly in his forehead.

Nazzir rolled cautiously off the roof of the visitor information stand at the Washington Monument. With a good rifle and a decent scope, it hadn't been a particularly difficult shot for a man of his skill. He'd been told to go the Museum when he was finished with his other assignments and wait to see if one particular man showed up. If he did, he was to kill him. Having done so, he broke the rifle down in the shelter of the closed concessions area. He carried the case over his shoulder and walked away from the fight to the Tidal Basin. A quick look around confirmed that everyone had fled the area, or gone to see what the shooting was about. With one quick movement, he tossed the case into the water and walked away, after sketching a brief salute to Thomas Jefferson in is Memorial across the way. He then set out a leisurely walk. He had a reservation at a Hyatt hotel not terribly far from here, and there was no rush. He'd finished what he needed to do today. It would have been easy enough to kill the law men who were mowing down the terrorists, but he hadn't been paid for that. Pity, the over all plan wasn't bad. But he didn't work for free. Making sure to swing wide away from the firefight, as it really wouldn't do to be hit by a stray round, he ambled off, the contentment of a job well done settling over him. When things calmed down a bit in a few days, he'd book a flight out, or maybe he'd just drive to Baltimore and leave from there. He mused over possible vacation spots as he made his way along the mostly deserted streets.

Several things happened at once, as they sometimes do in combat. The surviving terrorists realized they wouldn't last long in the open and that the trucks were no good as a point of retreat. Mark's anguished shout temporarily drowned out the shots, and the agents and officer reassessed their positions and options. Just as the attackers began sprinting for all they were worth for the doorway, the various law enforcement men began firing faster and harder. Several more fell as they raced for the door, but a few more made it. After they got inside, there was no longer a good line of fire for anyone. The shots ceased and a silence that seemed loud in the aftermath descended. Peering over the hood, Holmes finally yelled out "FBI, identify yourself!"

"DC Police" came back the answering shout. Craigson moved over to the downed Ariel as the two moved forward. Holmes drew back his foot to kick one of the downed men's weapons away, and Farris suddenly had what he'd almost call a flashback to earlier in the day (was that still today?). "Wait!" he said. Holmes looked at him, regarding the armored officer. "When we got the sniper earlier, his weapon was tied to a grenade pin or something, they kicked his gun away and everything exploded." Holmes nodded silently and they carefully checked the weapons before removing them, keeping an eye on the door in case the terrorists came back for another volley.

The two men murmured introductions and realized they had spoken at a remove earlier in the day.

Holmes secured the last weapon and they pulled the captured arsenal back toward the ruined SUV. "How's Ariel, Craigson?" Holmes asked. Craigson was kneeling next to her, and simply shook his head. "Awwww, shit," Holmes said and moved over to see her. It looked like the bullet had hit her gun, and ricocheted up at a bizarre angle, catching her perfectly between the armor plates. Her sightless eyes stared upward. Holmes worked hard to suppress all the emotion raging in him.

Farris looked away, to not intrude on the man's grief, and spied the other crumpled form. "Hey, who's that?" he asked, pointing.

Craigson moved over to the body and then said "Holy shit, it's Franklin."

"Paperclip?" Holmes asked, stunned. What had that desk jockey even been doing out here, and who had shot him without event taking a try at the rest of them?

Nabil was stunned. So few had made it? Truly, Allah was testing them most rigorously today. They were crouched behind one of the counters usually manned by volunteers to answer tourists' questions. Including himself, it seemed like there were only six of them now. He looked back out at the trucks. So close, and yet, they might as well be in Mecca for all the good they did them now. The plan had been to simply force an entry, make sure there were no stray armed security guards to give them problems, and then drive the trucks as close as they could and detonate them. Clearly, that wouldn't happen now. Whoever the interlopers were, they were well armed and incredibly accurate in their fire. Running for the trucks would be suicide, as opposed to martyrdom. There was no point in dying uselessly. He looked out into the lobby, at the huge American flag worked into the marble floor. They had wanted particularly to make it into the new gallery at the rear of the lobby where the flag called "Old Glory" was stored. He checked their remaining weapons. They could last a while, but they didn't even have any grenades. He wasn't sure if the rifle rounds would penetrate the case that flag was displayed in. He cursed, not seeing any way to complete their mission now. Perhaps he'd been overconfident, but he'd even left the control for the detonator in the truck on the front seat. No way to get there now, not that he could see. Was he being punished? Had he sinned against Allah in some way he couldn't fathom? He looked around again at the lobby—the entry and exit to the Old Glory Exhibit, the two stairs leading down, and the ways out to the east and west wings. Nothing came to mind, no inspiration struck, as to how to complete their mission.

The three left standing outside tried their various radios and cell phones to call for back up, or medics, or someone to care for the fallen, and no one was able to get through. Everything was down, or over burdened. Farris wasn't sure why his police radio wasn't getting anywhere, but supposed there was yet another trick in this string of attacks the terrorists had succeeded in today.

Holmes finally spoke. "Well, we can't leave them in there. And we don't have any idea when we can get help. Anyone have any ideas?"

Craigson looked at the vehicles in the street. "Well, I'd guess those are bombs, or full of explosives, or something. So let's not mess with them. Unless one of you has bomb squad training. I don't." Both men shook their heads. Holmes kept looking over at Ariel's still form. Craigson would never again believe the tales of the heartless bastard of an agent with a heart made from ice. "They haven't done any shooting since they got in there. Any ideas why?" Again, no one spoke up. "I'm out of ideas, but I'm the rookie. One of you come up with something." he said and moved over to the pile of rifles they had captured and began checking the various magazines and taking bullets from some to fill ones that were low.

"Hey, that's evidence," Farris objected.

"Later, after all this is done, it's evidence. Right now, it's ordnance. If we're gong to get something done here, we need all the help we can get." Craigson responded, continuing his reloading. Farris couldn't really argue with that, so he began helping.

Holmes found himself uncharacteristically at a loss. No brilliant idea was popping into his head. Nothing was suggesting itself. He looked over at Ariel again and then forced his eyes away. He'd grieve, but later. This wasn't the time. He moved over to the gear bag that Farris had put down while reloading and began to rummage through it, seeking inspiration. Farris looked over at him, but didn't speak, letting the man work. Finally, the bare bones of a plan started to form as Holmes found a few things he could use in the kit. "Ok, here's what we're going to do," he began.

Nabil al-Nadir wasn't sure what they were up to outside, but no counter attack seemed to be coming. Maybe they needed more orders from someone, or couldn't come into the Museum because of some obscure regulation. Perhaps they were more seriously wounded than he thought. Regardless, they could accomplish nothing by sitting here. Eventually, there would be more of them outside with better weapons, and they would roll right over his remaining men, maybe even using some of those robots he'd seen on one of those Discovery Channel shows. Those abominations were even worse than much of their culture of sex and ungodliness in Nabil's view. They were made to do a man's job, some even looking like men, and they moved. It was like idolatry combined with some even worse form of blasphemy. He shook his head to clear it of such thoughts. Now was the time for action. They were simply going to have to charge for that rear display area and see what the rifles could do. They could destroy the interactive display at the rear of the place easily enough, but he suspected that could be repaired almost as easily. This was supposed to be a blow to their ungodly hearts, not petty vandalism. He turned to his men. "Prepare yourselves. We go on my mark," he said.

The three men moved carefully up to the ruined doorway. Farris murmured to Holmes "They're not going to like this," mostly to take some of the nervousness off.

"The Smithsonian can fucking bill me if we live through it." Holmes whispered back. "Go."

Holmes and Farris fired into the entryway, past the shattered outer doors. The inner vestibule steered people to the right at a ninety degree angle toward the security station. Their volley of fire shattered the rear wall of the entry, not to mention startling the remaining terrorists as the sounds of automatic weapons fire coupled with shattering glass and reverberated in the vast lobby. Into this chaos Craigson threw what was left from Farris' kit of flash-bang grenades. As soon as the devices went off, they charged in.

Craigson called out "Clear left!"

Farris yelled "RIGHT, RIGHT, THEY'RE RIGHT!"

Craigson slid across the lobby floor trying to get out of their line of sight, knowing that most people with automatic weapons tend to shoot high. Holmes crouched behind one of the guard stations, while Farris backpedaled to the other side of doorway. Sporadic fire started as the combatants either recovered from the stun grenades or took up better positions.

What followed was furious and abrupt. Everyone started firing at extremely close range. Holmes dropped one man immediately and then fell back, catching bullets in his shoulder and leg, his own fire swinging off to the side as he fell. Craigson managed to catch two of them with a sustained burst before suffering several wounds himself and wounding one as he fell. The stuttering of gun fire warred with the metallic sound of shells hitting the floor. Farris fired at the group, hitting two more, one fatally. He was hit in the leg and the arm, dropping his weapon. Nabil smiled evilly, bleeding from a few minor wounds, looming over Farris. "You will die now." Farris scrabbled for his gun, breath hissing from the pain of his wounds, the gun out of reach. Holmes groaned but couldn't move. "All of you. And then we will destroy this place, and all the trinkets in it you fools value so highly." Farris tried again but couldn't reach it. The two inches might have well have been miles. "Why do you fight for them? You should be with us." Nabil said.

"Because Allah is Just, and Merciful, and despises murder." Farris spat out the words, expecting to die any moment.

"You have lost sight of what is Holy. Ask Him for forgiveness and maybe your soul will be spared." Nabil pointed his rifle at him and Farris silently said a final prayer for forgiveness for any wrong he had done and for failing at this last task.

The shot was thunderously loud. A corner of Farris' brain thought it was louder than it should have been, as adrenaline kicked in and provided that peculiar time dilation where everything slowed so far down. Then he saw Nabil flying through the air away from him, blood fountaining from his torso. A familiar voice came from the closest stairway. "Get away from my rookie, asshole."

Farris blinked, his ears ringing, and looked over at Rafe. "What are you doing here?" Rafe racked his shotgun, the spent shell landing closer to Farris than he would have liked.

"What, I was gonna let you have all the fun? I left communications when we finished talking to get over here." He checked the downed terrorists and moved their weapons away from them, cuffing a few that were actually still alive. "I came in the back and got caught up in all the staff running out. Then, I was working my way up the stairs when someone started tossing flash-bangs."

"Well it seemed like a good idea at the time," Farris rasped out, starting to realize exactly how much pain he was in.

Rafe, done securing prisoners and weapons, pulled out a trauma kit and began bandaging Farris, handing him a radio. "Here, keep trying with this, maybe you'll get through eventually." Farris began calling, repeating officers down, medics needed, over and over, eventually reaching someone, and starting a tidal wave of police, federal officials, medics and EMTs, and later media and then the curious as the building was taped off as a crime scene and the injured and dead were carried off.

Part of the legend of Nazzir was that he always wore grey. This was a carefully crafted fiction, like the Arabic sword marking he left on many of his victims when time permitted.

It was theatricality, and something else that helped tales about him circulate, which also let him charge more. Arriving at the hotel and collecting the bag he'd had sent in advance, he checked in and went to his room, changing into a casual khaki pants and blue shirt outfit. Using the computer in the business center, he did a bit of on line research, and finally decided on Barbados. He knew that his latest client, after all the mayhem caused that day, would quite possibly be trying to kill him as well to tie up loose ends. But since, as usual, he knew more about the client that the client did about him, he e-mailed him a sample of the damaging information that would be released to the FBI, DHS, and Associated Press in the event of his untimely death. Insurance arranged, he went to the lobby bar and ordered a scotch, relaxing.

Virgil Randolph looked at the readout. His machines had pinpointed a common point in many of the radio transmissions the terrorists were using. He overlaid the numbers on a city map, and produced an address. Looking up a few things about it, he put together a small packet of information and sent it as a text file to the cell phone of the cop who'd been in his lab earlier. Then, dismissing it from his mind, he went back to toying with a new design for a device that would be the size of one of the smaller cell phones, but have much better range, reception, and capabilities.

The medics were working on Farris, who had refused to go to the hospital. He'd been shot through the upper chest, narrowly missing a lung, and his left bicep, but avoided any serious wounds, although the EMT was not happy at his resistance. Craigson had a leg bone broken by a bullet, and few other various wounds, but would be fine in time with some possible reservations about the leg. Holmes had been grazed in the head, shoulder, arm, torso, and leg, and was being rushed to surgery. There was, of course, nothing that could be done for Ariel, or Franklin. Rafe stood off to the side, letting the medics work, miraculously unharmed. One photographer who had gotten on scene early took another one of the iconic images of the day, Farris hobbling to his cruiser, a bit unsteady on his feet, next to Rafe, who was ignoring most of the gun safety rules in existence, shot gun resting on his shoulder, while behind them Holmes was wheeled out on a stretcher.

Reaching Farris' car, Rafe looked over at him. "Ok, if you're not going to grow a brain and go to the hospital like a well trained officer, at least let me drive." Farris nodded and wordlessly passed over the keys, more than fine with slumping into the passenger seat. He was startled when his cell suddenly buzzed. YOU HAVE ONE NEW MESSAGE read the screen. He flipped it open as Rafe was saying "And really, what the hell time was that for a lecture? You were trying to piss off the guy pointing the gun at you? I know I didn't teach you that." Farris read the message, stopped, read it again, and blinked.

"We need to go somewhere." he said.

"Yeah, the ER, I was telling you that, along with the medic, remember?" Rafe answered.

"Pull over, or stop at least, and look at this." Farris shook the cell phone in his hand. Rafe, curious, stopped at the next red light and scrolled through the message.

Finally, he looked across at Farris. "Shouldn't we get some back up? Or at least some not shot-up help?"

"I want to end this. A lot of good people got hurt today. I saw I don't even know how many cops go down at the Old Post Office, and that Park Police guy at the Museum, and Hanson, and then us three got hit before you came in like the cavalry. Let's just do this." A look of determination crossed the younger officer's face. Rafe shook his head.

"You're gonna get me killed, kid," he said, but started driving to the address in the Northeast section of the city. Forced to use back roads and side streets, and sirens and lights at a few traffic jams, they made their way there. Farris did try a few times to get some help, but again, the radios were cutting in and out. Finally, in frustration, he forwarded the text to Joe Simmons, a guy he knew was working dispatch, and shrugged, then winced as his arm reminded him he was not in great shape.

Finally arriving, they regarded the street. It was south of New York Avenue, in a mixture of warehouses, small businesses, and a few buildings that weren't really identifiable at first, or even second, glance. Finding the right number, they moved along the loading dock of the warehouse to the office door. Rafe carefully reached out and tried the knob, finding to his surprise it was unlocked. They both exchanged nods and Farris counted down silently with his fingers: 3.2.1…and as he dropped the last finger, Rafe flung the door open.

The office was well decorated, looking like something out of a Middle East market more than a seedy warehouse. Behind the desk sat an overweight man in a suit, leaning back in his chair, a book open in front of him.

"POLICE, DON'T MOVE!" they both yelled, Rafe pointing the shotgun as Farris brought up his pistol in a slightly awkward one armed grip.

"Police? How banal. I was expecting Agent Holmes, or at least Franklin. Or are they indisposed?" the man asked, his low voice mocking. "Not even the FBI?"

"We're what you're getting." Farris said, eyes scanning the office. The man seemed to be alone, his hands were on either side of the book. He sat there, calm, a smirk on his face even, and Farris couldn't shake the feeling that something was wrong.

"Ah well, it's been a good day. I have seen on the news that the vast majority of what we tried to do was successful, although I'm less certain about the Museum. There don't seem to be any definitive reports on that."

"We stopped you. We were there." Farris said.

"Indeed? All that preparation for the various federal officials, and then it's the police of all people who upset the applecart. Ah, Insha'Allah." He shrugged.

"Put your hands on your head," Rafe instructed in a level voice, also picking up on the feeling that something wasn't right.

"Oh, I don't think so. I have no desire to be dragged through some dog and pony show of a trial with your commentators on the court house steps mouthing vague phrases some advisor told them to say. I am ready to make my exit." His right arm moved suddenly, reaching down below the desk, and both Rafe and Farris fired. The noise was deafening in the small space of the office, and the man fell over backwards, taking the chair with him, landing in a bloody heap. Rafe moved to check him, noting the large pistol that had fallen to the floor next to the man, and then shook his head.

"He's dead." Rafe said simply.

Farris sagged in relief, his aches and pains began to catch up with him. "It's over" he breathed out and let himself collapse in a chair.

Two Days After

Alejandro Valdez let himself into his brother's apartment. It was still hard to believe the smiling, charismatic, larger than life man was gone. He'd seen the endlessly repeated footage of the attack on the ball field, and smiled sadly as he thought of his brother's last act. Defiant to the end. He stopped at the kitchen counter and read the note, and thought that at least his brother's last night had been a happy one. Then he recalled where he had seen that name before, and his frown returned. She, too, was gone now. So many lives ended that horrible day. Alejandro shook his head and went back about his business, gathering his brother's papers for the inevitable issues with probate court about the will. A good bit of the money, he knew, was earmarked for a program to get sports equipment to various lower income school districts. He'd make sure this happened, and he'd get more donations, too. It was the least he could do for an idea that had been Hector's all along. He'd do this, in his brother's name.

Farris limped into Craigson' hospital room. The agent looked over at him and managed a weak smile. "Hey, good to see you." He gratefully pushed aside the mountain of paperwork on his bed tray. Even the hospital was no haven from the immense amount of paperwork he had to do, with discharge of weapons forms, post dated requisition forms for the equipment, the damage to the vehicle report, and many more.

"You too. Ah, the great white blizzard huh?" Farris gestured at the pile of paper. "I think I'm going to be writing until my keyboard locks up."

"Yeah, tell me about it. You catching any heat?" Craigson

asked.

"Well, a bunch of them are saying I went too 'cowboy' in what I did, but I think IA is going to have to go easy on me. The damn news thinks we're all heroes." Farris shrugged.

"I know, right? I'm getting interview requests from everywhere. But I'm hiding behind official policy and referring 'em all to the PR guy. I think he hates me about now." They both were careful to steer the conversation around the losses they'd taken, the ones they'd seen gunned down that day. Craigson laid back. "But I think if they ask me, I'm gonna do one with that Wanda Fullbright lady. You see her on the news?"

"She's been everywhere. She was actually there for some of it." Farris rose. "I was just dropping by after getting checked out." He raised his bandaged arm. "No lasting damage from the bullets, we just have to see how bad a hit my career took."

Craigson smiled back. "Don't sweat it, we're heroes, remember?"

"Hey, did you hear about that guy Rafe and I took down in his office?" Farris asked.

"I heard you nailed the mastermind." Craigson answered.

"Well, we think he was, but I just heard from the coroner's office, dude was way along in end stage cancer. Maybe he did all this because he figured he was on the way out." Farris said.

"Huh. Makes as much sense as anything else I guess." Craigson waved as Farris left, and then sighed, eyeing his pile of forms.

Ammar Hadad re-read the e-mail and glowered. Nazzir had been very careful in his safeguards, but then, so had Ammar. Issam Al-Mamdoh had been committed, as well as dying. He was the perfect scapegoat. Ammar liked to think he was fairly open-minded, and this particular idea had come his way years ago when he saw an American action movie, of all things. He couldn't recall now why he'd ended up ducking into the theater, losing a tail most likely. But he'd ended up staying, and towards the end, the villain, some German sounding man, had said something to the effect of "If you pull off something this big, they will keep looking, and they will find you, unless they think you're already dead." So, he'd kept an ear out for someone to take his place in the carefully stage managed finale. Still, he'd gotten most of what he wanted, and certainly repaid his brother's death many times over. "Rest well, brother," he thought, pondering his next move.

Two Years Later

Craigson, Farris, Holmes, and Rafe gathered silently. They were at Judiciary Square Metro station, which was surrounded by the low arcing granite of the Law Enforcement Memorial. Ariel's name, as well as LaSalle's, and the numerous other officers who'd died that day, had been added. They looked down at the names, remembering the events of the day. Holmes still had a slight limp, but he wasn't in the field much. From his hospital bed through his recovery, he'd traded on his "hero" status toward one goal, which was moving forward well. The information sharing idea he and Ariel had been working on informally for so long was becoming a real, recognized thing, with Holmes in charge of it. Aside from the organization itself happening, he'd also fought for the name, and had finally won that battle too. From now on, there would be a common pool of information for every member agency of DHS, and eventually all law enforcement if he had his way. It would be called the Hanson group.

Their Fates

If you think the story ended well on that note, stop here. You're done. It's all over. But, I wanted to give a few insights as to what happened to some of our cast here.

Wanda Fullbright became an accomplished news anchor and reporter, eventually going national, known for her human touch on many stories. Whenever she was complimented on her coverage of that terrible day in DC, she smiled a bit wistfully, remembering a lost friend and all those other people.

Bernie Holt won his share of awards also for the coverage of those traumatic events. He retired to Florida where he tried his hand at being a writer, discovered he wasn't, and took up fishing.

Nazzir remained something of a legend, until one day he just vanished. Rumor abounds as to what happened to the terrorist mercenary. Some say his old comrades did him in. Some say a rogue agent killed him, frustrated at never being able to prove anything against him. And some say he simply retired, possibly even becoming a novelist with unique insight into certain events, such as the attacks on Washington, DC.

Farris Fakhoury went on to a stellar career in the Washington, DC, Police Department. In light of his numerous accomplishments, the FBI approached him about a job. He turned them down, saying he was fine where he was, protecting his city as best he could. He eventually married, to his mother's delight, and had two children, a boy named Rafe and a girl named Ariel (this part, not so pleasing to the mother, but what can you do?).

Rafe Segovia was already known in the department, and

became legend after this day, if for nothing else than making it thought the shoot out at the Museum with no injuries at all. He eventually rose to Captain, and then later took a partial retirement, instructing at the police academy. There, he drilled Rafe's Rules into the new recruits as he once did while a Field Training Officer.

Mark Holmes made sure the Hanson Group was founded, financed, and became a reality. He worked as its leader for many years, making sure to recruit the best and brightest in computers, field work, and technical areas like bugs and monitors to keep the group on top. It eventually branched out to almost every major Federal agency, and many local law enforcement ones as well. He took early retirement when it was offered and later started a consulting group.

Bobby Buxton became convinced there was a reason he'd been spared, even in such a humiliating fashion as his "lechislators" comment that was all but forgotten about in the wake of the attacks. He stopped drinking, began going to church, and eventually became a reverend, preaching especially on the values of humility and dedication. He started a low ranked television show, which grew slowly, and he became a nationally recognized face of religious authority. He will tell the story of how he was saved to anyone who asks, but has managed to remain open minded and humble, doing great works behind the scenes in many poor neighborhoods.

About the Author

Wayland Smith is the pen name for a native Texan who has lived in Massachusetts, New York, Washington DC, and presently makes his home in Virginia. His rather unlikely list of jobs includes private investigator, comic book shop owner, ring crew for a circus (then he ran away from the circus and joined home), deputy sheriff, and freelance stagehand.

Wayland is a four time participant in, and survivor of, NaNoWriMo, having made the 50,000 word goal each time. A black belt in shao lin kung fu, he is also a fan of comic books, reading, writing, and various computer games (I'll shut Civ down in one more turn. Really). He lives with a beautiful woman who was crazy enough to marry him and a goofy dog with a fondness for peanut butter and white wine.

Look for these books
from Blue Oranda Publishing
in your favorite e-bookstore

By Harry Heckel

Crimson Hawks Adventures
In the Service of the King
Cinders and Ashes (Coming Soon)

Krueger Chronicles
Souls of the Everwood
Black Powder and Brimstone (Coming Soon)

Charming (with John Peck) (Coming Soon)

By Brad A. White

Servant of the Muses

By Dara Hannon

Broken Faith